Your Hotel Room

*that morning I found myself wanting to stay
but I couldn't." Brandon gazed into her eyes
as he spoke. "I left the rose in my place. I
waited for your phone call until midnight,
when I called you. The first thing I intended to
tell you was my real name. I was going to tell
you the truth, and explain what I was doing on
the bridge—"*

"Playing a game," Elaine snapped.

MONICA BARRIE,
a native of New York State, has traveled extensively around the world but has returned to settle in
New York. A prolific romance writer, Monica's
tightly woven emotional stories are drawn from
her inherent understanding of relationships between men and women.

Dear Reader:

There is an electricity between two people in love that makes everything they do magic, larger than life. This is what we bring you in SILHOUETTE INTIMATE MOMENTS.

SILHOUETTE INTIMATE MOMENTS are longer, more sensuous romance novels filled with adventure, suspense, glamor or melodrama. These books have an element no one else has tapped: excitement.

We are proud to present the very best romance has to offer from the very best romance writers. In the coming months look for some of your favorite authors such as Elizabeth Lowell, Nora Roberts, Erin St. Claire and Brooke Hastings.

SILHOUETTE INTIMATE MOMENTS are for the woman who wants more than she has ever had before. These books are for you.

Karen Solem
Editor-in-Chief
Silhouette Books

Distant Worlds
Monica Barrie

Silhouette Intimate Moments
Published by Silhouette Books New York

America's Publisher of Contemporary Romance

SILHOUETTE BOOKS
300 E. 42nd St., New York, N.Y. 10017

ISBN: 0-373-07001-2

First Silhouette Books printing February, 1985

10 9 8 7 6 5 4 3 2 1

This one is for my friend,
Bill "Uncle B." Milla
M.B.
Spring Valley, N.Y., 1984

Chapter 1

THE COOL NIGHT AIR BRUSHED ACROSS ELAINE'S FACE, bringing with it all the varied scents of the city. The gentle breeze filtering from the confluence of the East River and New York harbor lent a warmth to what could have been a chilly fall evening.

Elaine remembered New York from the many times she and her parents had visited it, and she had always found the city both exciting and vital. The feeling that permeated the atmosphere filled her mind and made her glad to be a living and breathing being.

Taking a deep breath, Elaine crossed the large intersection known as Confucius Square and walked toward the nearby Brooklyn Bridge. She had treated herself to a delicious dinner at Hung Loo's, one of the many great restaurants in New York's Chinatown. But afterward Elaine had felt the need to walk and think. Her mind was a foggy mess of confused thoughts that not even the five-and-a-half-hour plane flight had been able to sort out.

The streets were busy, though not jammed with people, and her progress was quick toward one of New York's most famous symbols. Reaching the foot of the bridge, Elaine saw the tourist area was dark, and glanced at her watch. It was later than she'd thought and she realized her body was still working on west coast time.

Elaine avoided the dark patches; instead, she followed the cement walkway that led to the pedestrian crossing of the historic bridge.

Although she had no intention of crossing the bridge she wanted to stand above the river and look out at it. At that hour the walk was deserted, though the roadway itself was still clogged with traffic.

Elaine stopped to peer over the railing. Spread out before her was the magnificent and fabled skyline of lower Manhattan. Lights from a multitude of buildings flickered with a majesty that was purely New York's own, and, gazing at the splendor of the city, Elaine appreciated the differences between New York and Los Angeles.

It was colder on the bridge than on the city streets, and Elaine drew her sweater more tightly about her as she continued to stare out at the city. Soon the sparkling lights faded from before her eyes as her mind again turned to her troubled thoughts.

She had arrived in New York less than four hours earlier and, after checking in at the Inter-Continental, had made several phone calls. Then, her stomach growling hungrily, she'd taken a taxi downtown to Chinatown. But it was none of these things that took her mind from the beauty before her. Elaine's confusion was the very reason for her being here in the first place.

In the four years since she'd graduated from U.C.L.A., she'd worked for Trion Studios, first as a production assistant and then, a year later, as an assistant producer. She'd worked hard since she'd received the promotion, and had been a part of five films, from inception to completion. But, three days ago, just after she'd seen the edited version of the last film she'd worked on, everything had changed.

In her office at the studio, Elaine hung up the phone and took a deep breath. The phone call had been a summons to David Leaser's office, and David Leaser was the highest of highs, the president and chairman of the board of Trion Studios.

Could something have been wrong with the film she was working on? Elaine wondered. She'd gone over the final edited version the night before, and it had looked very good. *No, it must be something else.*

Rising, Elaine left her desk, went into her small private bathroom and checked herself in the mirror. Her makeup was still fresh and the gray suit fit nicely, complementing her figure but not calling undue attention to her five-foot-eight height. Her light brown hair shone with streaks of natural blond, enhanced by the layering of her above-the-shoulders haircut. Her blue eyes, sparkling in her tanned face, needed little makeup. Using her fingers, Elaine combed her hair, then left her office.

Though she appeared calm on the surface, Elaine couldn't help being nervous. She'd only been in her boss's office twice in four years and both times had been far from pleasant experiences. The first summons had occurred when she and the producer she was working with had run way over budget on a film and the second had been because of production delays.

Elaine passed a poster for the first movie she'd worked on and smiled to herself. She'd come a long way in four years, but she knew it was only the beginning.

And I have a lot more hard work ahead of me, Elaine thought. She knew everyone watched her constantly, waiting for her to make a mistake so they could point their fingers, and say "I told you so." But Elaine wouldn't let that happen. There was pressure on everyone in the movie industry but, as the daughter of one of Hollywood's great producers, Lawrence Rodman, it was especially difficult for Elaine.

From the time Elaine was able to understand movies, she'd wanted a career in the entertainment industry. At first she'd thought it would be acting, but as she grew older, she realized the behind-the-scenes action was what had caught her interest and imagination. She'd studied directing, but learned that her interests leaned toward the production, not creative, end of films. By the time she'd graduated from college, Elaine knew that she wanted to be able to work in all aspects of moviemaking, to be able to handle every phase of film production completely.

In her four years with Trion, she'd learned a great deal, and hoped to produce her own film within the next year. With that in mind, Elaine turned the corner of the poster-studded hallway and arrived at David Leaser's office. Opening the door, Elaine stepped into the richly appointed office of David's secretary, Jennifer Dalton, who had started at the studio at the same time as she.

"Am I in trouble?" Elaine asked before she'd even closed the door.

Jennifer smiled and shook her head. Masses of white-blond hair rippled with the movement. "Yesterday he was in a rotten mood; today he's okay."

"That's not what I asked."

"I know, but you'll have to wait until you speak to him. Go ahead in, he's waiting."

"Thanks," Elaine said as she started toward the far door.

"Lanie," Jennifer called. Elaine paused to look back at her. "Good luck."

Puzzled by Jennifer's words, Elaine knocked lightly on the door and opened it. Inside the elegant yet simple office of David Leaser, Elaine waited for a signal of recognition from the man.

"Good morning," Leaser said. He pointed to a leather couch across from his desk.

"Good morning," Elaine replied as she sat down on the cool leather.

"I hear *Office Girl* will be a money-maker."

Elaine nodded. "I just saw the final print. It looks very good."

"Ron says you worked your tail off."

"I did my job."

"After four years, don't you think you can take that chip off your shoulder?"

Elaine took a deep breath, then slowly shook her head. "No matter what I do, everyone points their finger at me and says 'That's Larry Rodman's kid,' they don't say 'That's Lanie Rodman.' "

"So what if your father's famous? You can't help that."

"It's not that, it's the fact that every time someone looks at me, I sense that they think I got my job because of him."

Leaser shook his head slowly before he spoke, his voice

low and intense. "We both know that being Larry's daughter opened the door for you, just as we both know that the door would have slammed shut in your face if you couldn't have done the job. I think it's time you tried to ignore what you *think* other people are saying about you. Lanie, it's time for you to get above that and move on in the industry."

"Move on?" Lanie echoed.

"Yes. How would you like to produce a movie for me?"

Startled, Elaine stared openly at him. Several seconds later, she began to breathe again. "Do you think I'm ready?"

"We wouldn't be discussing it if I didn't think so," Leaser informed her dryly.

"What movie?" she asked, trying to control her sudden excitement.

"Distant Worlds. Preproduction is almost underway; all I need is the nod from you."

Elaine remained silent for a moment while she digested his words and thought about the movie. She'd heard about it several times and thought the idea was a good one, but she also knew that the production staff had already been set. "Isn't Tom Sellert the producer?"

"He was, but I pulled him. We had 'artistic differences.' Do you want it?" he asked bluntly.

It took Elaine all of half a heartbeat to nod her head.

"Good. There's just one thing I want you to know. It was you, not your father, who got you this far in the industry."

"Thank you," Elaine said honestly.

That night, Elaine celebrated her newest promotion by taking her father out to dinner. They ate in a small restaurant overlooking the Pacific, and Elaine told Larry Rodman about her new film. Her father was genuinely happy for her, and he refrained from giving her advice, for which she was more than grateful. After dropping her father off, Elaine drove to her small house on the outskirts of Malibu, and spent most of the night reading the script in preparation for the next day's work.

Elaine moved into her new office, complete with secretary, the next morning and threw herself head on into the new project by looking over everything that Thomas Sellert had done so far.

All the contracts for the actors had been signed, and Elaine was excited to see that a friend, Cindy Reed, was set to co-star in the movie. The arrangements for sets and locations had been made already, which freed Elaine from a lot of work and allowed her to plunge fully into the technical aspects of producing the movie.

On the second day of the new assignment, her assistant producer, Jason Heller, had come into the office with bad tidings—Allen Marshall, the star of the movie, had been in a freak motorcycle accident and would be unable to work for at least eight months. Marshall had suffered facial burns, and it would take a long time for the burns to heal enough for plastic surgery to be performed.

Elaine knew Allen, and immediately sent him a card and a large bouquet of flowers. Then she had her secretary call David Leaser to schedule an appointment.

At five o'clock, Elaine was again sitting on the leather couch in David's office, waiting for him to finish his phone call. When he hung up, he turned to her and smiled.

"What do you know about Brandon Michaels?" he asked.

"Nothing. Who is he?" By the expression on Leaser's

face, Elaine knew she should have been familiar with the name.

"Brandon Michaels is one of the hottest properties in New York. He's doing the lead in *Lifelines* on Broadway and last year he won a Tony for best supporting actor in a drama."

"Last year, I was the assistant producer of two-and-a-half films and spent nine months overseas, seven in Italy and two in France. I don't remember having the time to attend a Broadway play, or even to watch the Tony awards. Has he done any films?" Elaine asked, wisely tempering her sarcasm with the question.

"There are English-language newspapers in both countries, and no, he has not made any films. He has successfully avoided the lure of Hollywood. From what I understand, he considers himself a *serious* actor."

"Then why are we discussing him?" she asked.

"Because Simon Arnold, the man who wrote the screenplay of *Distant Worlds* also wrote the play Brandon Michaels is starring in. Arnold originally wanted Michaels for the part, but Michaels turned it down."

"And now?"

"When we found out about Allen's accident, I called Arnold. He said he'd speak to Michaels about it, and he did. A half hour ago Brandon Michaels agreed to take the part," Leaser said proudly.

"Why did he change his mind?" Elaine asked.

"Because he and Simon Arnold have become friends, and Simon promised him the screenplay would accurately reflect the writer's philosophy."

"You're kidding."

"No. I agreed that there would be no shooting-script changes without Arnold's, and Michaels', approval."

Elaine couldn't believe her ears. Unknown actors and screenwriters just don't tell a studio what to do. "Why?"

"Because this is a pet project of mine. I believe in the movie, and I'll do whatever is necessary to make it a success."

"Is that why Tom Sellert isn't the producer? Did your 'artistic differences' necessitate the change in producers?"

"Lanie," Leaser said in a low, warning growl.

Elaine shook her head slowly. "I've known you all my life, and I know you're a fair man. That's why I came here for a job. I think I have the right to know the answer to my question."

"You're as stubborn as your father. All right, to answer your question, yes. Sellert and I disagreed about the project, and I offered him another movie."

"Offered or ordered?"

"In my position, they're tantamount to the same thing. Now why was it so important to you?"

"Because I'm in the spotlight. I've already heard the rumor that it was I who got Sellert canned."

"There are always rumors floating around; what people say can only hurt you if you let it. I think it would be a lot simpler if you just produced a movie good enough to shut up the jealous people."

"That's easy for you—"

"Don't cop out on me, Lanie, just show the world what you're capable of, okay?"

Elaine looked at her father's close friend for several long moments before she nodded her head.

"Good!" Leaser declared. "Tomorrow I want you on a plane to New York. The contracts will be ready in the morning, and I want you to see your new star in action."

"Excuse me?" Elaine said, taken aback by his words.

"You're going to the opening night of Brandon Michaels' play. I want you to see him in action and tell me what you think of him as an actor."

"Is it necessary?" she protested. "You've already decided on him, and I have a million things to do to get production started."

"Yes, it is necessary," David Leaser stated with finality.

And so Elaine found herself on a plane to New York, to see just what the star of her first movie was like.

The sound of two voices pulled Elaine from her thoughts. She blinked her eyes and once again saw the splendorous skyline of New York, but her confusion stayed with her, even as the couple's footsteps receded.

No, she ordered herself, refusing to give in again to worry and self-doubt. She had accomplished a great deal in the four years since she'd started in the movie industry, and she wouldn't let the fact that she had no choice in the casting of her first movie discourage her or interfere with her determination to prove herself equal to the task.

Drawing in another deep breath, Elaine glanced toward the Brooklyn side of the river, and at the slightly less picturesque skyline there.

As she tried to clear her mind, she thought she heard another voice. Elaine looked around but saw that she was alone on the bridge. Concentrating, trying to block out the traffic noises, Elaine listened intently. Then she was sure there *was* a voice and, surprisingly, it was coming from above her.

Leaning against the railing, Elaine peered up into the

inner construction, but could not see a thing. But as she did, the voice grew louder, and she listened to what it was saying.

"You are beautiful, and you are sad. You make me want to stay here and look upon you daily, but you offer me nothing of your reality to see. No, you stare at me, with your cold, cruel eyes, and challenge me to love you. I do. But you give nothing in return."

Elaine shivered at the chilling depth of the man's voice. Its deep timbre and resonant tones were clear and rose above the sounds of the traffic on the bridge. Forcing herself to be quiet, Elaine continued to listen.

"What is the point in going on? Why should I bother to drag myself through the days when I have only the nights to face again? The night is cold, lonely and empty without you, and it brings only the return of the day. Another aimless day that will be filled with the nothingness of life itself."

A warning chill crawled upward along Elaine's spine, and she sensed that what she was hearing was not a farce, not some eccentric man playing games on the bridge. Elaine suddenly realized what was happening, but was afraid to say anything. At the same time, the magic of his voice held her captive. It wasn't his words, but the very essence of his magnetic voice that drew her to him.

"Would I not find a better place, a warmer nestling, in the waters below? It calls to me, like a siren waving her undulating arms. Yes, the siren of the water calls me to join her in an embrace. I want to press my head to her breasts and give of myself for an eternity. For the water asks only one thing, that I give myself to her, and nothing more. She makes no demands upon me, she asks only for my love. Yes, tonight I shall join her, and say good-bye to all that is familiar. For with familiarity there comes loneliness and deceit.''

Elaine was rooted to the spot. Fear flooded her mind and turned her legs to lead. The man's voice had sliced through her, his plea, his litany, had pierced her to the heart. She too had known loneliness and deceit, and it had taken her three years to forget. But now she was filled with life and couldn't bear to think of someone who was not. The depth and resonance of the man's voice was too beautiful to be denied. It would be a terrible crime for it to be silenced forever by the cold waters swirling beneath the bridge.

Yet Elaine knew she mustn't do anything rash. She should go for help, find a policeman who knew how to deal with this type of situation. Before she could take a step, the man's voice rang out again, louder than before, and Elaine was again frozen to the spot.

''Yes, I will come to you. The time is now, for if I wait longer, my resolve will be lost. I come, beautiful darkness, to be with you.''

As she listened to him, time ground to a painful halt. The intensity of the moment distanced her from everything and everyone but the man with the beautiful voice.

''No!'' Elaine cried, unable to stop herself from intervening. Bending over the railing, she twisted herself awkwardly and stared upward, searching for the body behind the voice. ''You can't.''

''What?'' he called, and Elaine knew she had taken him by surprise, and that that could be dangerous.

In college, she had studied psychology, to prepare herself to work better with the various personality types she would find in the movie business. Now, as she talked with this strange man, she remembered the several case studies she had read on suicide. Elaine knew that she was doing everything wrong, and that knowledge frightened her badly, but she couldn't keep still.

"You have no right to do this. You mustn't," she yelled, trying again to see the man above her. In this new position, she was able to discern a form, but not its features. Then she heard him laugh.

"No right? I have every right to do as I want!"

"You have no right to do this to me!" Elaine said, irrationally angry that the man was arguing with her, and afraid, at the same time, that she would be unable to stop him from his foolishness.

"Go away; leave me alone."

"Only if you come down," she said. Her heart was pounding furiously and her breathing was rapid as she wondered why she was doing this. If he didn't want to live it was none of her business. But there was something in his voice that called to her, some quality she didn't understand. Intuitively, she knew one very important thing: There was something special about him.

"Why?"

"Because what you're doing is wrong."

"You don't understand I'm no—"

"I understand. I've been there, too, but I learned that there was more to life than ending it. Please come down," she pleaded.

"Would you believe me if I said I wasn't trying to commit suicide?" the man asked.

"Come down and prove it," Elaine challenged.

"I don't have to prove anything to you," he said.

"I thought you said you weren't really trying to commit suicide?" Elaine countered, knowing the man was lying, and hoping that she could make him leave the spans of the bridge. "Now prove it."

"All right," he said at last.

She hadn't realized she'd been holding her breath until she heard her own sigh as she exhaled. She watched anxiously as the man extracted himself from the girders and worked his way down to the walkway, emerging eight feet from her. When he was safe, he turned to stare at her. His face was lit by the overhead lights and, once again, Elaine's breath caught.

He was at least six-foot-one, with a full head of dark, curly hair. His face was handsome, yet even though it was, Elaine sensed the man cared little for his looks. Even in the dark, Elaine saw that his body was lean and powerful, and emanated a life force that denied the act he had been attempting only moments ago. Forcing herself to breathe normally, she tried unsuccessfully to break the hypnotic hold his eyes had on hers.

What color are they? she wondered illogically.

"Why did you stop me?" he asked in that deep, magical voice.

"How could you even think about killing yourself?" she asked, ignoring his question.

"There are a lot of reasons for someone's taking his life and most of them would be none of your business. But thank you for caring," he said as he started forward.

She knew he was about to walk past her and out of her life, and she suddenly didn't want that to happen. "Wait."

The man paused and stared at her.

"At least tell me your name."

"That could be a mistake. The Chinese have a saying

about what you've done tonight. Are you sure you want to know?''

"Please."

"Paul."

Elaine laughed nervously as the tension slowly began to drain from her. "You don't look like a Paul," she said inanely.

"Believe me, *tonight* I'm a Paul."

"What do the Chinese say about what I've done tonight?"

"That when you save a person's life you become responsible for that person for the rest of your life."

"I've heard of that before, but I never knew you had to know the person's name first."

"You don't, but I thought I'd give you a chance to back out."

Elaine realized that what was happening was ridiculous —standing on the Brooklyn Bridge, bantering like a silly fool with a man who'd just tried to kill himself—but she was too intrigued to turn her back now.

"Paul," Elaine began, but paused for a moment as she gazed into his eyes and saw that they were green, sea green. "You won't try to do this again, will you?"

"You do care, don't you?"

Elaine held his gaze and slowly nodded, because it was the truth.

"I'm finished killing myself for tonight," he said in an almost amused tone. "But—"

"No buts," Elaine said, cutting him off and extending her hand to him. "Lanie."

"Hello, Lanie," he replied, taking her hand in his.

Elaine almost gasped when their hands met. He'd

grasped her hand tightly, and a branding heat raced upward along her arm. When he finally released her hand, she thought her arm was on fire. Staring at him, Elaine tried to understand what was happening to her, but as soon as she'd gained control of her emotions, she shivered under the assault of another sensation. This one she recognized, and knew it resulted from the tensions of the past minutes.

Taking a deep breath, she forced herself to smile. "Well, since I'm now responsible for your life, can I buy you a cup of coffee?" she asked.

"Why?"

Elaine was again the object of his intense scrutiny, and again at a loss for words. An eternity seemed to pass before she found her voice.

"Because I've never saved anyone's life before, and I want to sit down for a few minutes until I stop shaking," she said truthfully.

Paul reached out and drew her to himself. "I'm sorry," he whispered.

Elaine suddenly found herself in a secure embrace and, even though he was a stranger, she did not fight what was happening.

"Come," he commanded as he released her, only to take her hand and lead her toward the New York side of the bridge.

They walked silently. Elaine was totally aware of his hand on hers. She could feel both the strength of his grip and the heat that radiated from his hand. By the time they reached the street, the trembling that had shaken her had gone.

"Where do you live?" Paul asked as he attempted to hail a cab.

"Los Angeles," Elaine responded.

"You traveled three thousand miles to rescue me?" he asked with a grin that revealed sparkling white teeth.

"Hardly," Elaine replied with her own smile.

"Where are you staying?"

"The Inter-Continental," she told him just as a cab pulled to the curb. Once they were seated, Paul gave the driver the hotel's name, and they were off. Silence descended in the backseat, and Elaine was afraid to speak, afraid to say anything. The strange, ethereal mood that had followed Paul's descending from the girders was still with her, and there was something else as well, something she didn't recognize.

When the driver stopped in front of the hotel, Paul thrust a ten-dollar bill into the man's hand as the doorman opened the cab's door. He followed her out, and when they were standing together in front of the hotel, he spoke again.

"Still want the coffee?"

"I think I may need something stronger," she replied.

"I agree," he said. Taking her arm, he guided her into the luxurious hotel, and then into the ornate lounge.

Chapter 2

"THANK YOU," PAUL SAID AS THE ELEVATOR DOOR opened.

"You're welcome," Elaine whispered, casting her eyes away from the mysterious green depths within his. Withdrawing her room key from her purse, knowing that she had no choice, she started toward the waiting elevator.

"Lanie," he began, but Elaine raised her hand to stop him, the room key gripped tightly within it.

"I'm glad we met, and I'm glad I was able to help. Have a good life, Paul," she said in a barely audible voice before she quickly slipped into the elevator. She stared at him until the doors closed.

The ride up seemed to last forever, and it was only after she was inside her room that she breathed a sad sigh of relief. The night had taken its toll on her, and she was looking forward to sleep. Opening the closet door, Elaine glanced at its meager contents.

One dress and two business suits hung there, accompanied by her favorite light robe, a silk kimono her father had brought back for her from Japan. The small amount of clothing would meet her needs for the two days she was scheduled to be in New York.

Elaine undressed and put on the robe. After washing, she went to the large club chair and sat down on it with her long legs thrown carelessly over the arm.

She closed her eyes, but opened them quickly when she found Paul's green eyes suddenly staring at her. *Stop!* she ordered herself. Elaine knew she didn't need anyone else's problems, least of all the problems of a man who hadn't wanted to go on living.

In the lounge, she had studiously avoided talking about what had happened earlier. Their conversation had been light, but the tension that permeated the air between them had been almost palpable. Each time their hands brushed on the table little electric shocks had raced through her. His eyes had held hers in bondage for long minutes, and Elaine had not wanted succor.

But she knew that her promise to herself wouldn't permit anything to happen between them. Once had been enough, and that one time had driven her to the very edge of sanity. Earlier, on the bridge, she'd been telling Paul the truth when she'd told him she'd understood, that she had been there before—she had. Although she hadn't contemplated suicide, she had thought her life to be over.

It had been a beautiful love affair—at least she had thought so—and she'd willingly given of her love, her loyalty and herself. She had been engaged to Malcolm Stewart, one of the up-and-coming young directors at Trion Studios. They had started dating a month after she'd started working there and three months later he had asked her to marry him. She had agreed, happy beyond belief until that fatal day, three years ago.

It had been lunch time, and she'd had an hour break from filming. She'd picked up two box lunches at the studio commissary and gone to Malcolm's office. When she'd arrived, she had found the outer office deserted. Shrugging her shoulders, she'd gone directly to his door, which was ajar.

Turning, she had pressed her back to the door to open it because her hands were full. But before she did, she'd heard voices and froze. Malcolm was talking to someone, and she hadn't wanted to barge in. As she had listened, her happiness had turned to grief.

"Of course I'm sure I'll be able to pull it off," Malcolm had said.

"He's not stupid," replied a familiar voice that Elaine had recognized as Jeannie Daniels's, one of the young starlets from Malcolm's last movie.

"Neither am I. I promise you that in three months the contracts for your new movie will be ready, and I'll make you a star!"

"As long as *she* doesn't find out," Jeannie had said.

"She won't. She's in love with me, and I've got her wound around my finger. We'll be married in two months, and I'll have Larry Rodman eating out of my hand too!" Malcolm had boasted proudly. "Enough talking for now. Come here. I want you."

With the harshness of her fiancé's words ringing painfully in her ears, and the sickening insolence of his faithlessness all too apparent, Elaine had stepped away from the door. Her breath was tortured and her heart felt as if it had stopped. She had gone to the secretary's desk in the outer office and thrown the two box lunches on it. Then, conscious of the tears spilling from her eyes, she'd left the office and gone to the first bathroom she could find. There, behind a locked door, she had cried endlessly. But later, when she had emerged from the bathroom, the only trace of her sorrow was the redness of her eyes.

She had returned to her own office and had forced herself to work hard throughout the day. When she'd left work, she'd driven straight home, locked the door and spent the night alone, refusing to answer the phone's incessant ringing, though she had known it was Malcolm.

The next day she had called in sick, the only time she had done so since she'd started working at Trion, and had gone to see her father. In the home where she'd grown up, she'd told her father what she'd discovered, and had looked to him for advice and sympathy. The advice she'd received had been wasted on her at the time, and the sympathy was hardly what she'd expected.

It was not until much later that she learned to appreciate what her father had said to her. "Lanie, you're not a little girl anymore, you're an adult. You fell blindly in love with Malcolm. Now you must live with your eyes open."

"But I love him," she'd said. "How could this happen?"

"Lanie, you and I and others like ourselves, in the entertainment industry, live in a different world. Men like Malcolm Stewart and women like Jeannie Daniels are a part of that world. You have to learn to look deeply into these people's souls before you make a decision that changes your life.'' Larry Rodman had turned to look at the portrait of his wife, Elaine's mother, and had gazed at it for a long moment. ''One day you'll meet the right man, and when you do, you'll know it.''

''We're not in a cliché-ridden old movie, Daddy. I just want to know why.''

''Lanie, I'm sorry, but you were, as the saying goes, prime bait.''

Her father's words had shocked and hurt her almost as much as the conversation she'd overheard the day before but this time she had stood her ground and glared at her father.

''Why are you doing this to me?'' she had whispered, holding back her tears by the strength of her fast-dissolving willpower.

''Because I love you, and because it's time you saw the world as it is.''

''Daddy—'' She'd tried to deny his words, but her mind had mercifully shut down. A second later, she'd felt herself engulfed in her father's strong arms, and stayed there until her spasms of grief had eased.

When she'd left her father, she had driven to the coast. She'd stopped at a spot overlooking the ocean and had stood on the edge of a cliff, watching the swirling, powerful waves crash against the rocks. It was then that, had she been a weaker person, she would have thrown herself into the rushing waters to ease her heartache.

And although that thought had flashed through her mind, Elaine knew that she wouldn't take the easy way out. Suddenly the strength to face the world had returned, and she had known that in the future she wouldn't take anything, or anyone, for granted.

Elaine had made a promise to herself that day, and it was an easy one to keep. There would be no other men in her life until she reached the point in her career that she was struggling toward. She would devote herself to her work and avoid falling into foolish traps like the one she'd just found herself in.

With her decision made, Elaine had returned home. There, she'd gathered everything that Malcolm had ever given her and had packed it in a large box. She'd put the box in the trunk of her car and driven the ten miles to Malcolm's house.

He was not at home, and Elaine decided that she would leave the box at his front door. With that accomplished, she had gone home, to prepare herself to face work the next day, and to face the rumors that would be floating around by the time she got there.

Malcolm had shown up at her door that night. When Elaine had opened it and found him there, she had stepped outside to tell him that she knew everything. Malcolm had tried to lie his way around it, but Elaine hadn't given in.

"We're finished, Malcolm. Go back to your starlet," she'd flung out at the end.

"You're making a mistake, Lanie. Don't blow a good thing."

"I'm not, but you did. Good night . . . and goodbye." With that, Elaine had stepped into the house and closed the door on Malcolm Stewart forever. Those parting words had become the cornerstone, the foundation of the walls she had built to protect herself from hurt. With each passing day, Elaine had built her defenses brick by brick. But even as she did, Malcolm had haunted her dreams. The love she had given him so freely had become bottled up inside her only to erupt in painful waves whenever she was the loneliest. Yet Elaine had refused to give in to her sadness, and over the months and years she'd grown strong again. Neither did she forget how she had been used, nor did she forget her promise to herself.

Elaine took another breath and forced her thoughts from the past back into the present. Glancing at the small digital clock beside the bed, she saw it was past midnight. "Time for sleep," she told herself aloud. But she didn't move as yet another picture of Paul surfaced in her mind.

What terrible thing could have forced him to attempt that desperate act? she asked herself. In the two hours she'd spent with him, his strength and magnetism had shone like a coat of armor, denying the weakness to which she had been an audience. Elaine hadn't once felt the need to question him about the reasons that had driven him to the bridge. By the time she had signed the check, over Paul's protests, she had pushed the memory of the incident into the back of her mind.

Now, alone in her room, the more Elaine thought about him, the more she felt that Paul's desperate act wouldn't be repeated. Downstairs, in the lounge, he had been so vital, so full of animation and life that she'd found it almost impossible to equate him with the man on the bridge.

Once more, Elaine tried to take her mind off the handsome man, but again she failed. Shaking her head, Elaine admitted the truth of her feelings. She had been attracted to him as she had never been to another man. She knew that if she hadn't forced herself to say good-bye to him in the lobby, everything she had tried to accomplish for herself, all her promises and goals, might have gone by the wayside. But the memory of his closeness, of his masculinity flooded her mind. The long moments when he had held her tightly on the bridge; the heat of his hand on her arm; the silent messages his eyes had sent her, all combined to bring out a sense of loss for the man she would never see again. "Have a good life," she'd said when they parted. Now Elaine regretted the flippant way she'd spoken.

Elaine stood quickly as she tried to dislodge dangerous thoughts by physical action. She was about to leave a wake-up call when she realized she wasn't expected at the Trion office before noon. Shrugging, Elaine clicked off the overhead light, leaving on only one lamp to illuminate the room. She turned down the quilt in preparation for sleep, but before she could take off the kimono, there was a knock on her door.

She was caught off guard, and before she realized what she was doing, she was at the door. Just as she grasped the knob, she stopped herself. This was a strange place, not home, and she knew better than to open the door to strangers.

"Yes?" she asked as she leaned close to the door.

"Lanie, it's Paul," came the deep, melodious voice, its strength undaunted by the thickness of the door.

"Paul . . . what?" she asked, surprised by this new development and by the racing of her heart.

"I need to talk with you," he said.

"I was just going to bed."

"Please, Lanie, it's important."

Elaine paused for a moment. There was nothing in his voice that reminded her of the earlier moments at the bridge, and she detected nothing to be afraid of. Elaine

opened the door and stepped back, her hand unconscious-
ly holding the top of the kimono closed.

"Thank you," he said with a smile that reached all the
way to his eyes, making the crow's feet at their corners
spring into life.

"You're welcome, I think," Elaine said, as relief filled
her at the way he was gazing at her. From the instant he'd
entered the room, his eyes had stayed locked on hers, not
dropping to her silk-draped body.

"Lanie, I'm not the type of man who beats around the
bush. I was halfway home when I realized that I had to
come back and explain about tonight."

"You don't have to explain. Leave what happened in
the past, where it belongs."

"Lanie . . ."

The way he said her name sent goose bumps rising
along her spine. She found herself falling into the depths
of his eyes, lit so gently by the low light of the single
lamp. *Stop!* she ordered herself, but her body wouldn't
obey her mind.

"Paul, no, please," she whispered.

"You're beautiful," he said in a low voice.

Elaine's breath caught at his words. She felt as though
his eyes were caressing her. The myriad emotions she'd
been subjected to this night assailed her senses, and the
tension returned with a powerful impact. So much had
happened tonight, so many feelings had been called
upward in her mind.

"I . . ." she began, but his face was close to hers, and
his warm breath washed across her cheek. His arms were
around her, drawing her close. She remembered his
embrace on the bridge, and the sudden security she had

found in his arms. Then his lips were upon hers, and a shock of desire exploded in her chest.

A long moment later, Paul released her. "From the instant I saw you on the bridge, I wanted to kiss you."

"Paul—"

"Let me finish. I know you don't want an explanation of what happened tonight, but one day you'll have it. Lanie, tonight is a special night for me, a new beginning, and I want to share it with you."

Elaine stared at him for a moment, trying to silence the throbbing of her blood. His words had struck a deep chord within her, and her heart welled toward him although her mind reeled with confusion.

He released her as suddenly as he had embraced her. "I'll leave if you want me to," he whispered in a husky voice, his eyes holding hers in a steady gaze.

Elaine knew that the decision must be hers. She had spent three years controlling her emotions, warding off any and all attempts to get past the barriers she had erected, but tonight those barriers were ready to crumble. She knew that if he as much as touched her again, she would lose her good sense. But while she wrestled with her emotions Paul did not move, did not touch her.

Elaine's throat constricted and she slowly raised her hand to stroke his cheek. The moment her hand touched his skin, she was lost. Then his hand was on hers, and he drew her palm to his mouth, covering the tender skin with warm kisses, his eyes never leaving her face.

With the suddenness of a summer thunderstorm, Elaine's barriers fell and, with a small cry that was both denial and acceptance, Elaine went into his arms. Their lips met in a terrifyingly deep, soul-wrenching kiss that left her weak and holding on to him for support. The kiss lasted an eternity while the fire within her chest spread to engulf her entire body.

Logic and reason fled. Her blood turned to lava, her arms wound around his broad back, and her hands pressed it tightly.

Then his hands were wandering along her back, firm and smooth as they traced the contours beneath it. When the kiss ended, their joined intake of breath sounded loud in the silent room. Elaine gazed at him, afraid to speak, afraid to move. She had never before felt such an onrushing of desire.

Elaine wanted to cry out, to stop what was happening, but when she opened her eyes, she saw the need reflected on his face was the equal to her own. *Madness,* she told herself even as her eyes closed and their mouths joined again.

Elaine was lost in the kiss and the masculine strength of Paul's arms. Then he moved, sliding one arm down as he turned and lifted her off her feet. She felt herself floating and held him tighter as he walked.

Elaine tried once more to summon up the words to stop this insanity but failed, and buried her face in his neck. Her senses were assaulted by the heady male scent clinging to his skin.

Then they were at the side of the bed. Paul, instead of placing her on it, released her and held her against his body. His lips covered hers and his strong hands held her tightly to him. At that secret place deep within her, she felt her need for him grow.

Their lips parted, and Paul stepped back. His hands went to her shoulders and slipped the kimono from them to expose their tanned slopes. Slowly, Paul continued to ease away the robe, until at last it was crumpled at her feet, and he was gazing unashamedly at her.

"You are truly beautiful," he said, his voice husky. His eyes caught hers, and the intensity of his gaze sent yet another rushing wave of desire through her. With that desire came a feeling of vulnerability so powerful that her legs threatened to collapse. But mixed with the passion that was controlling her, was the need to speak to him.

"Paul, I have to tell you . . ." Elaine began, her eyes never leaving his, but she couldn't find the words. She had just met him, yet they were about to—

"Nothing, you have to tell me nothing," he said in a low voice. Elaine stared at him and saw that he did understand what she couldn't say aloud.

They continued to gaze at each other until Elaine could stand it no longer. She raised her arms to him, and the handsome man came back to her. Their lips met, and this time the kiss was deeper, even more passionate than before.

Then they were on the bed, and she was tasting deeply of Paul's mouth. Elaine returned his ardent kisses fervently, giving as much as she was taking, and again time slipped away.

Paul moved, taking his mouth from hers. It was gone for only a heartbeat before Elaine felt his burning lips on the curve of her neck. Her hands wound into his hair, weaving through the thick mass of curls, as a moan escaped her throat.

Through the pulsing of her blood, Elaine was conscious of the heat of his lips trailing along her neck, igniting fire after fire in her already burning body. His hands caressed her skin and she gasped as his hand cupped the soft mound of her breast. She almost cried out again when his thumb outlined her now erect nipple and his mouth raced across her skin.

But as quickly as the sensations came, they stopped. Paul was suddenly sitting up and staring at her. Elaine's chest was tight, and she was afraid that she would faint under the deep stare of those sea green eyes. Miraculously, Paul smiled softly, and Elaine knew that everything would be all right.

He rose gracefully, and Elaine watched him begin to undress, but as soon as his shirt was open and she glimpsed the broad expanse of his chest, she closed her eyes.

A moment later, with her eyes still closed, she felt him return to the bed. His mouth touched her forehead then roamed downward along her cheek, until it reached her soft and pliant lips.

Then his hand was on her breast again, caressing it gently before his mouth followed his hand, and another low cry was torn from Elaine's throat. Pinpricks of fire covered her breast, and her back arched in response. He shifted again, and his mouth was on her other breast, lavishing it with kisses and caresses, until her mind swam with the magnificent sensations.

Elaine was aware of the unreality of the moment. She was in a dreamlike state where time stood still and the outside world receded until the here and now became the only thing that mattered. Elaine's hands began to wander along the muscles of his back, her fingernails outlining its breadth. Her heart beat loudly, and the liquid fire that was her blood boiled as never before.

His lips returned to hers, and within his strong embrace, Elaine could no longer think; instead, she returned his caresses with her own, her mouth seeking his, kissing the sweet-tasting lips before leaving them to travel along his neck. His hands were like burning embers as they stroked her, and his lean body, pressed to hers, was molten fire.

Amid all the sensations assaulting her, Elaine was very much aware of the tremendous need building deep inside her, a need that cried out for release. Her hands roamed his back of their own volition, exploring the lines of his body. His skin trembled beneath her touch, and she felt the tensing of each muscle that her fingertips traced. Suddenly she was lost in the feel of him, and in the gentle yet strong way his hand caressed her.

In a whirlwind of movement, Paul grasped her firmly and eased her onto her back until she was staring into his handsome face. Then his hand moved to her cheek to cup it for a moment before he lowered his mouth once again.

When their lips met another cascading rush of heat spread through her, and she cried out when he pulled his mouth from hers. The room swirled madly as his mouth dropped lower, tracing a fiery trail to the peak of her breast. The pinpricks of fire returned to blanket her tender skin and the volcano that was rising within her began to smolder.

Paul lifted his head and stared deeply into Elaine's eyes as he moved upward along her body. When his mouth was a bare inch from hers, her arms went around him and her legs slid along the outside of his thighs. Suddenly, she felt the heat of his manhood against her, and she was all too aware of how badly she wanted him.

He entered her slowly and carefully, filling her. Elaine

tensed as the branding heat of his manhood sent lances of
lightning shooting deep within her. When she stiffened,
Paul paused. His mouth went to hers, and their tongues
met and danced the waltz of love. The tension eased from
Elaine's body and Paul, slowly and gently, began to carry
her on a voyage of passion.

Their bodies molded together and their hearts beat in
unison. From deep within her, the volcano erupted,
turning her blood into lava and sending her thoughts flying
to a distant place that had no name, as she moved in
harmony with this powerful man.

Elaine let him lead her on, guide her on this journey of
discovery. The power of his body seemed to flow into
hers, giving her more and more strength, until another
fiery explosion shook her, and her body trembled against
the leanness of his.

Elaine cried out again and she tightened her arms and
buried her face in his shoulder as yet another wave of
passion was released from deep within her very core.

Then she was helpless, carried along by his powerful
body until she felt him tense and explode deep within her
warmth.

For endless moments they lay together, neither willing
to move, their breathing loud in the quiet room. But at last
Paul lifted himself from her, only to return to her side and
draw her close to him. They didn't speak and Elaine was
glad for that because she felt shaken to her very soul. To
hide it from him, she kept her eyes closed and her face
tucked between his shoulder and his neck.

But even with the strange mixture of emotions that held
her in its grasp, she luxuriated in the warmth emanating
from his body and in the soft caresses he lavished on her
back. Soon the tensions that had been a constant part of

her for so long began to ebb. Before she realized it, Elaine was asleep, wrapped securely within Paul's arms.

Elaine rose through an ever decreasing fog until she could open her eyes and see the bright red light of the bedside clock. It was four-thirty. She lay her head back down and tried to remember where she was. Then she turned and gazed at the barely visible features of the man she had made love with a few hours before.

A wave of warmth washed through her and the feelings of doubt that attacked her lessened. She had no excuse for what had happened last night, but intuitively knew that it had been right. Slowly, carefully, she leaned over Paul and grazed his lips lightly with her own.

He stirred, then his eyes opened. "I guess I fell asleep," she whispered.

"We both did," he replied.

"Paul . . . I . . ." Elaine saw a shadowy smile form on his lips. She blushed, and was glad it was so dark.

"It's all right, everyone falls asleep."

Elaine felt the beginning of a nervous laugh, but held it back and shook her head. "How did you find my room number?"

"You told me."

"I . . . excuse me?"

"When you said good-bye to me at the elevator you were holding your key. I saw the room number on the tag."

"Oh . . ."

"I'm not a very sinister person," he said in a low voice as he reached up to cup the back of her head.

Elaine moved with him, and lost herself in the taste of his lips. But this time there was no great upsurge of passion; rather, a gentle warmth spread to enclose them both. She moved slowly, freeing herself from restraint as she explored and learned her lover's body. After countless caresses and kisses, they joined together again, and Elaine was carried to another peak of passion that left her clinging tightly to his broad back.

It was an hour before sunrise when Elaine fell back to sleep, but just as she reached that floating plateau that invited dreams, she was struck by a new thought. For three years she had denied herself any emotional involvement, yet in the space of a few hours she had gone back on all the promises she had made to herself about falling in love.

No! the word echoed like a scream in her mind, and she forced it from her thoughts. *One night in a man's arms is not love,* she told herself.

But sleep could not be denied, not even with frightening thoughts roaming errantly through her head, and finally Elaine joined the handsome man again, this time in sleep.

Chapter 3

A THIN STREAM OF SUNLIGHT FILTERED THROUGH AN edge of the closed curtains and roused Elaine from her sleep. Stretching, Elaine opened her eyes and glanced at the clock. It was almost noon. She turned to look at Paul.

Her breath caught and a wave of sadness spread through her when she saw that he was gone. But when she looked at the indentation his head had left on the pillow, she saw something else. Lying in the exact center was a blood red long-stemmed rose.

Reaching over, Elaine lifted the rose and brought it to her nose. She inhaled the sweet essence and her eyes misted as another wave of sadness spread through her.

He was gone, she realized, and she didn't even know his last name. Then another thought struck her, chasing away the sadness, replacing it with a hot rush of shame. She was thinking of the abandon and wantonness that had ruled her mind and body last night.

How could I have done that? she asked herself as she clutched the rose's stem tightly in her hand. *Fool!* she named herself bitterly, every detail of the night returning to taunt her cruelly. She had done the one thing she had vowed never to do. She had become involved with a man, and a stranger, at that.

What could have possessed her to react to him that way? she wondered, forcing her body to rise from the bed. But the memory wouldn't leave her thoughts, and with it was a vision of Paul. Everything had seemed so right between them.

In all her twenty-five years, Elaine had never let herself go the way she had last night. It was not in her nature to be so free with her body, or her mind. She tried to analyze what had happened, and realized that last night had been filled with such a vast range of emotions that she had not been as firmly under control as she usually was.

She knew she was troubled about her new job, the lack of control she had over the casting of the movie. And that, combined with Paul's attempt to end his life, had overloaded her already heavily burdened emotions.

Stop rationalizing! she ordered herself. From the time Elaine had grown into womanhood, she had made it her business to be honest with herself and not hide behind false pretenses. Even if what she had surmised was true, it was still no excuse for what had happened last night.

But no matter how hard she tried to chase away his handsome image, Paul's face continued to float boldly before her eyes. She could almost feel again the masculine strength that had poured from him to enclose her in a safe cocoon, chasing away any doubts that she'd had.

And yet another even more disturbing thought edged its way into her mind and Elaine felt an unreasonable stab of fear. Last night, before falling asleep, she had wondered why she was so attracted to this stranger. "No, it can't happen this fast," she whispered, refusing to even think of the possibility. "Besides," she said to the rose, lifting it to sniff its fragrance, "I'll never see him again."

She knew her last statement to be true, for there had been no note with the rose. *I must put this behind me*, she told herself with steely determination.

With her mind firmly made up, Elaine rose and left the bed to prepare for the day ahead, knowing that she must submerge herself in work in order to keep from thinking about Paul—or the night before.

It was six o'clock when Elaine stepped from the cab and entered the lobby of the Hotel Inter-Continental. She went to the front desk and checked for messages. Although she expected none, four years of working on film locations had instilled this habit in her. More than once she had found important messages awaiting her that she hadn't expected.

The desk clerk disappeared for a moment, and when he returned he handed Elaine a sealed envelope with her room number scrawled on its face.

Rather than open it in the crowded lobby, Elaine walked toward the elevator, conscious that she had less than an hour to get ready. Curtain time was at eight, and she wanted to take a shower before putting on her evening dress.

She had put in a full afternoon of work, and had spent over two hours on the phone with her assistant producer, who had called about an emergency. One of the locations that had been prearranged had fallen through, and they needed an alternate site for two of the movie's scenes.

When Elaine had finished with him, she had been called
into a meeting of east-coast distributors, and introduced as
Trion's newest producer.

She had acquitted herself well, and the men had seemed
impressed with what she'd had to say. When that meeting
ended, she had met with the director of operations for the
east coast, Sy Margold, to discuss not only her present
project, *Distant Worlds,* but two of her past movies as
well. Near the end of their talk, Margold had asked if she
was excited at the prospect of working with Brandon
Michaels.

"I've never seen his work. In fact, I've never even seen
a picture of him," she'd admitted.

"And I thought that everyone in Hollywood knew
everyone in the 'business,' " Margold had joked. "I think
I have his picture in here somewhere," he'd added as he
began to search through a drawer in his desk.

"Don't worry about it, Sy, I'll see him in the flesh
tonight."

"Ah!" Margold had exclaimed when he found an
eight-by-ten glossy and extended it to her.

"You can't tell much from the picture. He's costumed
as Arthur. He did *Camelot* last year; this is a publicity
photo of him during the second act."

Elaine had taken the photograph and studied it carefully. Brandon Michaels was fully costumed in a flowing
robe that covered him from neck to toes. His hair, unless it
was a wig, was dark and straight, and reached below his
shoulders. His heavily made-up face, and a thick, partial
beard and mustache accented the virile look of the period
in which the play was set.

She'd given his face another moment's study before

returning the picture to Margold. Something about the man was familiar, but she was uncertain what it was. Perhaps she had seen his picture before in the newspapers.

"Is the beard real?" she'd asked.

"He grew it for the part."

"Yes," Elaine had said, "he's a *serious* actor."

"He's also a damned good one," Sy Margold had stated firmly. "Both David and myself have spent the last year trying to sign Michaels for a film."

Elaine had heard the reprimand in Margold's voice, and realized that he was an admirer of Brandon Michaels. That in itself said something to her, because, as a rule, most film executives didn't go overboard about actors.

"I'll certainly find out tonight, won't I?" she had asked in a pleasant tone.

Sy Margold had glanced at his watch, and then at Elaine. "If you make the curtain in time. It's a quarter to six."

Startled that the day had flown by so quickly, Elaine had thanked Margold for his time and left the office for the hotel, where she'd found the message waiting.

With the envelope in her left hand, Elaine opened the door to her room and went inside. It was only when she saw that the maid had straightened up the room, and had even put the rose in a glass of water, that she allowed herself to think of Paul and last night.

Throwing her purse onto the bed, Elaine looked at the envelope. It bore the emblem and logo of the hotel, but she didn't recognize the handwriting. Using her thumbnail, she opened the back flap, and withdrew a single folded sheet of paper. As she began to read it, she gasped. It was from Paul.

Lanie, you looked so beautiful in your sleep that I couldn't find it in my heart to wake you. I had to leave, but when you can, please call me at 555-2354.

"Why?" she asked the note, even as the bold and distinct handwriting blurred before her eyes. Blinking rapidly in an effort to control her emotions, Elaine crumpled the note and flung it away.

"You should have woken me!" she said. Turning, Elaine began to undress, but before she could take off her blouse, she found herself staring at the crumpled note. Trying to ignore it proved impossible, as another vision of Paul's face danced within her mind.

Shaking her head in defeat, knowing that she was about to make a fool of herself, Elaine retrieved the note, opened it and went to the phone.

What will I say to him? she asked herself. *How can I speak to him casually?* But although she was unsure of what she would say, she knew she must speak to him and hear the magic of his voice. As her finger reached for the dial, Elaine froze. *Leave last night in the past,* she told herself. It was the same advice she'd given Paul when he'd tried to explain himself to her.

Taking a deep breath, Elaine willed her hand to reach the dial. *Relax,* she advised herself. She dialed the number and, three rings later, heard a click on the line. She recognized Paul's voice instantly when he said hello.

"Hello," she replied nervously.

"You have reached 555-2354 and, as you can tell, I'm not home."

"I hate tape machines!" Elaine yelled into the receiver, more out of nervousness than anything else.

"Please leave as long a message as you want, and I will get back to you as soon as possible. Thank you."

A moment later she heard the electronic beep, and spoke. "Paul, this is Lanie, and it's a little after six. I'm off to the theater, but I'll be back by midnight. Please call me if you can."

When she hung up, she wondered if she had sounded casual enough. Then she wondered if she'd been too casual. She hoped her nervousness wasn't too apparent.

Elaine finished undressing and took her shower. Twenty minutes later, wearing her kimono over her bra and panties, she put on the finishing touches to her makeup. After drying her hair and brushing it into a swept-back style, she went to the closet and took out the dress she would be wearing that night.

Opening night at the theater was an exciting event, and most people dressed up for it. Elaine had brought a lovely cocktail dress of blue silk, embroidered with white satin thread.

The dress was a wraparound type, with a thin belt that secured it at her waist, emphasizing its slimness while also showing the smooth outward flair of her hips. The bodice was crisscrossed, and although it hugged her breasts, it wasn't really provocative. The hem was of an uneven handkerchief design, which permitted flashes of her tanned calves to show whenever she walked. Then Elaine slipped into three-inch heels and took a matching wrap from its hanger, settling it on her shoulders. Hopefully the material would keep her warm enough on the ride to and from the theater.

Glancing at the clock, Elaine saw that she had spent more time dressing than she'd expected, and that the curtain was due to rise in only twenty minutes.

Moving quickly, she picked up her purse and then paused. Without knowing why, she reached for the rose in its glass of water. With a smile, she decided to take it too.

The taxi let her out at Forty-sixth and Broadway, unable to get through the crowded street where the theater was located. After paying her fare, Elaine walked toward the theater, then paused to study the marquee. *Lifelines* was proclaimed in big bold letters, and Brandon Michaels's name was only smaller by a slight degree. On Broadway that meant a great deal; it told the world the status of the play's star.

But would he make it as a movie star also? she wondered as she worked her way through the milling crowd in front of the theater.

It was a typical opening-night crowd, made up of celebrities, theater critics, the people in the higher echelons of the social strata, and of course, the obligatory television camera crews.

Walking quickly and extracting her ticket from her purse, Elaine skirted the first television crew and joined the crowd entering the theater. To her left she saw a network anchorman wave to the crowd lining the street, while New York's mayor was being interviewed by one of the newscasters and, behind him, she saw Tony Randall sidestep yet another television reporter.

Elaine handed her ticket to the usher, and after he'd returned the torn half to her, she took a few steps into the lobby, then stopped in her tracks.

This opening was a bigger event than Elaine had realized, and the multitude of tuxedo-clad men and women in evening gowns was more than she had been prepared for. Elaine looked around for a friendly face, but saw no one she knew. The low roar in the lobby of the theater sounded like the onrushing waves of a stormy ocean as they reached the shore.

The excitement of opening night could be felt in the tension-filled atmosphere. Elaine overheard varied comments and guesses about whether the play would be a success or failure.

"Miss Rodman," called a voice from the crowd. Elaine turned to see who it was, and she recognized Philip Casey, one of Trion's distributors, who she had met at the meeting that afternoon.

"This is a surprise," she said as she extended her hand to him.

He took it in a firm grip and smiled at her. "I've had tickets to this opening for months. I wouldn't miss it for the world. Where are you sitting?" he asked.

Elaine glanced at her ticket and then at him. "C-eight," she said.

"Good seat, third row, center aisle." As he spoke the lights blinked once in the lobby. "Last call," Casey said with a smile. "If you have no plans for after the show, I'd love to take you to Sardi's. It's another great show," he said with a knowing wink.

"Thank you, but I did make other plans. Enjoy the show," she added quickly, covering her lie with a smile. She had no other plans, but the predatory glint in Philip Casey's eyes was warning enough to stay away. Besides, the last place she wanted to be in was Sardi's, the famous after-theater restaurant where a large crowd went to await the reviews of their plays on opening night.

Without her realizing it, the lobby had almost emptied. Elaine followed the last of the crowd inside, and presented her ticket stub to the usher. As the distributor had told her, it was indeed a good seat from which she could see the stage clearly. The usher handed her a Playbill and Elaine glanced at the cover and then opened the program. Just as she found the page with the cast photos on it, the lights went out, music filled the air and the audience fell expectantly silent.

Wishing she'd had time to at least see Brandon Michaels's picture, Elaine sat back and looked at the stage. The velvet curtains parted slowly, revealing two actors standing in the center of the stage, lit by pinpoint spotlights that illuminated only them.

There was a smattering of applause to greet the actors, but by its low volume, Elaine knew that neither of the men was Brandon Michaels. Usually the star of a Broadway show received a big hand upon his first entrance.

Elaine tried to make out what the set looked like, but because of the fuzzy darkness, she could not see it very well.

Surrounding the actors, and above them, was what appeared to be the lines of an erector set. But, as her eyes adjusted to the darkness, she thought she recognized the set as something familiar. Then she saw what she thought to be a huddled figure sitting on one of the pieces of the erector set, but she wasn't quite sure. Elaine gave up her inspection and listened to the lines the actors were speaking.

She found she couldn't concentrate on the play. Again her eyes swept the darkened set, until a chilling sense of recognition stirred in her mind. Then she understood what she was seeing. It was a set designed to look like the structure of a bridge.

The Brooklyn Bridge? Elaine shook her head forcefully, but was unable to dislodge the thought. Once again she concentrated on the actors, willing herself to hear their words.

"I hope he can get *her* here in time," said one actor, his voice filled with desperation. He looked toward the side of the stage, and then up into the inner construction.

"He will, dammit, he will!" declared the second man.

Elaine wondered what was going on, and chastised herself for not learning more about the play and its storyline. Then another spotlight came on, and within it was a woman. The audience applauded loudly, and Elaine joined in to greet Brandon Michaels's co-star, Elizabeth Sandor, who was presently riding a wave of successful plays, her last one earning her a Tony nomination. Behind her came yet another actor.

"Sondra," called the first actor, "thank God!"

"This had better not be some joke," she snapped harshly.

"I don't think death is much of a joke," the first actor retorted.

"You really are serious, aren't you?" Sondra asked, looking from face to face. "When this *goon*" she said, pointing to the actor who had accompanied her onstage, "came to my apartment and told me what was going on, I refused to listen to him until he forced me to come with him."

" 'Forced'?" asked the first man.

"That's what I said," she replied caustically.

"She wouldn't come. She told me to tell Paul to get it over with and leave her alone," said the third actor.

"You're a cold bitch!" snapped the second man.

Just as the actress turned to face the man who had spoken, Elaine absorbed the name the actor had just used. *He had said Paul.*

Just the coincidental mention of Paul's name sent a rush of emotion through her mind, making her lose her concentration.

"If I'm so cold a bitch, why am I here?" the actress asked. "Where is he?"

Elaine watched, fascinated by what was happening, even though she didn't yet understand the basic premise of the play. She saw two of the men point upward into the darkened set, and she almost cried out when a disembodied voice floated from the darkness.

It took every last ounce of her strength and willpower to sit still, because she had recognized the voice instantly. *It can't be,* she said silently, but the unseen actor continued to speak, and Elaine felt herself being transported back in time to the night before.

"Yes, Sondra, you are cold. But you are beautiful, and you are sad. You make me want to stay here and look upon you daily, but you offer me nothing of your reality to see. No, you stare at me with your cold, cruel eyes, and challenge me to love you. I do. But you give me nothing in return."

Elaine's stomach convulsed, and for a moment she thought she would be sick. The heat of her shame turned her skin to fire, and her hands twisted the program to shreds.

But as ill as she felt, she couldn't stop listening to the very scene she had been a part of last night.

"We had a good love once, but it's over, Paul, and nothing you can do can change that," Sondra said.

"Yes, there is something I can do. Look below you! Look at the pure water. Would I not find a better place, a warmer nestling, in the waters below?"

"Stop playing the fool and martyr!" Sondra yelled.

"A fool I must be, for the water calls to me, like a siren waving undulating arms. Yes, the siren of the water calls me to join her in an embrace."

A row of spotlights came on, flooding the upper level of the set with light and pinpointing the exact location of the actor who had not yet been seen. The audience was silent, so caught up in the play that they did not applaud the play's star, nor would it have been appropriate if they had.

But Elaine, sitting not more than thirty feet from the stage, saw Brandon Michaels for the first time. Nausea filled her and Elaine forced herself to close her eyes. *Brandon Michaels was Paul!*

Fool! Stupid, asinine fool! Elaine called herself. Then a sharp pain tore through her hand, and she glanced down, opening it. The program fell away to reveal one lone thorn from the rose's stem imbedded in her palm.

Letting the pain clear her mind of the treachery she had just witnessed, Elaine took several deep breaths, and the nausea began to recede. She no longer heard the magical, resonant voice of Brandon Michaels. She had shut everything from her mind except the need to escape.

Her first impulse was to stand and shout out a denial, to tell the man what she thought of his deception, but her common sense came to bear, and she knew she wouldn't make a spectacle or degrade herself in public.

Instead, Elaine rose quickly and walked from the theater, ignoring the startled glances of the people she passed. Only when she was outside, standing on the sidewalk, did she breathe easier.

She stared at her hand, at the thin line of blood that ran from where the thorn had pierced her skin. Balling her hand into a fist, Elaine shook her head. *It doesn't matter,* she told herself as she began to walk. She saw nothing, nor did she remember having crossed a single street, but somehow she had returned to the Hotel Inter-Continental, and she found herself alone on the elevator, riding toward her floor and the safety of her room.

Inside the room, Elaine tried to think of what to do. He had made a fool of her. He had used her, made a conquest with lies and then left her. She knew now that he would never call, that he would listen to the message she had left on his answering machine and laugh at her.

Suddenly all the ramifications and complications of the past days welled up in her mind. Surmounting it all was the fact that she would have to work with Paul—*no, Brandon,* she corrected herself. *Impossible!*

Elaine stared at the bed where she had spent the night before, and a shudder passed through her body. She knew she couldn't spend another night in this room. Moving like one possessed, Elaine took off her dress and threw it on the bed. Next, she pulled out the garment bag and began to pack, leaving out a business suit to wear, not caring how she put anything into the bag. When the bag was packed and she was dressed again, she called the airline. She changed her return flight from tomorrow at eleven to the midnight flight tonight. Then she called the front desk and informed them that she was checking out. Forty minutes after walking out of the theater, Elaine signed her charge slip and left the hotel.

The doorman signaled to a taxi, and only after she was seated in the back and the driver had pulled away, did she sigh with relief.

She would be home early tomorrow morning, and she would be safe there. *Safe from what?* she wondered, but she knew she would never be safe from the pain and heartbreak she was now suffering, the empty aching feeling that called all her denials lies. No matter how many times she told herself she couldn't have fallen in love with him, the truth reared its head and haunted her with its knowledge.

The after-theater rush was almost claustrophobic as Brandon Michaels pushed through the crowd. He felt a heady exhilaration from the performance, brought on by the knowledge that everything had gone well. The audience had given the entire cast a standing ovation that lasted through seven curtain calls. When the curtain descended for the last time, the cast itself had turned to him to single him out with the same enthusiasm the audience had so generously lavished upon them all.

Elizabeth Sandor, his co-star, had kissed him on both cheeks, and his friend Simon Arnold had wrapped Brandon in a joyful embrace. But as soon as the cast began to leave the stage, Brandon went to his dressing room, changed quickly and inconspicuously left the theater before anyone else.

Opening nights were a strange phenomenon. Most actors dreaded them before the play started, and afterward spent hours sitting at a restaurant table, awaiting the reviews—agonizing over whether the play, and their own performances, would be accepted.

Brandon had learned early in his career not to give in to these apprehensions. He preferred the solitude and quiet of his apartment. He never watched newscasts on opening night, and only when he woke in the morning would he look at the papers. But Brandon had the ability to know by the time the play was halfway through whether or not it would be a success. And *Lifelines,* he knew, would make it. The play felt right, and he had sensed, with the intuition of a true actor, that the audience had been fully drawn into the drama, and had stayed with it until the final curtain fell.

But tonight Brandon was restless, which made him want to break his habit of solitude and share his elation with another. Brandon also realized there was only one person he wanted to see tonight, but he knew he must call her first—he couldn't just go to her hotel. There were explanations owed to Lanie, and that would be his first priority.

He signaled to an approaching cab, and, after giving the driver his address, sat back to watch the crowded streets pass by outside the window.

When the driver reached Central Park West and Eighty-second Street, Brandon had his wallet out. A block later the cab pulled to the curb, and Brandon handed the driver the money. The cabbie turned to him with a smile.

"How did it go tonight, Mr. Michaels?"

"Great, thank you," Brandon said as he waited for his change.

"Mr. Michaels, could I trouble you for your autograph? Me and the wife are fans of yours."

"No trouble," Brandon replied with a friendly smile, and took the autograph book the driver had produced from thin air. He asked the driver's name and his wife's, and wrote a small note to them. Brandon didn't mind doing this; he accepted it as part of acting.

"Thanks, Mr. Michaels," the driver said when he took back the book and handed Brandon his change. "I'll see you next week. I got my tickets two months ago."

"Wonderful," Brandon replied.

Brandon crossed the street and entered the lobby of his co-op. "Evening, Mr. Michaels," said the doorman.

"Evening, Peter," he replied. Taking out his key ring, Brandon went to the waiting elevator and inserted the key into a slot near the top of the elevator's buttons. One of two lights lit up, the one marked PH-2.

The elevator opened directly into his foyer, which was decorated in soft earth colors. This apartment was his haven, his private world, hidden high above the city that had been so good to him.

Walking through the living room, Brandon didn't glance at the modern, modular couches. He didn't see the breathtaking view of the city from the large picture window, nor did he stop to admire one of his favorite possessions, a print of Cézanne's *Water Lily,* which occupied the center of one white wall. Instead, he went straight to his den, which was also his office, and looked at the answering machine with its red, blinking light.

"Did she call?" he asked the recorder. Since he had left Lanie that morning, she had been rarely out of his thoughts. But he'd forced himself to concentrate on his preparations for opening night. At eleven this morning, he had gone down to the lobby, bought a rose and written a note that he had left with the desk clerk. Then, after placing the rose on the pillow next to hers, he had gone to the theater for the cast meeting. Following that had been unending interviews with the press and then another cast meeting, in which they went over the material again.

Before he'd realized it, the day had been gone, and he was in his dressing room, clearing his mind, getting ready for the performance.

Brandon pushed the rewind button on the answering machine, and a moment later it clicked loudly and began to replay the messages. Most of the calls were good-luck wishes, but the seventh call was the one he was waiting for. When he heard Lanie's voice, his pulse accelerated.

Glancing at his watch, he saw it was just a little after eleven, and he would have to wait until twelve to call her. He took off the light jacket he had worn home from the theater and sat down on the leather swivel chair. Resting his feet on the matching ottoman, he leaned his head back and closed his eyes.

A picture of Lanie surfaced in his mind. He recalled every detail of her face, from her large, light blue eyes, to the way her hair seemed to sparkle, as though it were sprinkled with gold.

The throaty tone of her voice, the softness of her pliant lips and the way she had looked at him combined to send lances of desire surging through him. *What a strange way to fall in love,* he thought. But Brandon was one of those rare people who could accept the unusual and sometimes unexpected happenings in life. This trait was reinforced by his strong determination and an inherent understanding of who and what he was.

Brandon's memory brought back the events of the night before with crystal clarity. For Brandon, it was just as if they were happening again. He remembered the full impact of his shock upon hearing her voice while he rehearsed alone on the Brooklyn Bridge.

He smiled at the ludicrous position he had found himself in on the bridge and at his inability to explain to Lanie who he actually was and what he had been doing on the bridge. He had only realized after they had joined together and shared their bodies, that he no longer wanted to play the role he had started the evening with. He wanted to tell her that what he had been doing was so much a part of his life that at times he almost forgot who he had been before he'd turned to acting.

When Brandon had decided that being an actor was what he wanted, he had thrown himself into his new career with the determination that had always been a part of him. Brandon Michaels had been born Brandon Winslow Michaels III, and had grown up one of the pampered rich—a fact he had so far hidden from the press and public.

His father had refused to force Brandon to follow the same path as his friends, who were content to live and follow in their parent's footsteps. He preferred instead to show Brandon just how much of the world could be his if he wanted it and was willing to work for it. By the time Brandon entered college, majoring in computer science, he was determined to show his father that he could do anything he set his mind on. After receiving his masters degree, Brandon borrowed money from the trust fund his mother had set up for him and started his own computer consulting firm.

Although the money was legally his, he drew up loan papers and treated it as a regular business transaction. Brandon wanted to prove to himself that he could become successful without the money he was heir to. At the age of twenty-five, with the loan of $120,000 repaid, including interest, Brandon Michaels was a millionaire. At that point Brandon had hired the best men to take over his business and had gone into other ventures, always successfully.

But the one thing Brandon had denied himself, in his pursuit of business success, was the balancing effect of a real social life. Belatedly, Brandon began to date frequently, but he rarely went out with the same woman more than three or four times. For some reason the women he'd met all seemed to be fawning creatures, incapable of being themselves in their efforts to impress him. The one thing he always looked for but never found was a woman with a true sense of herself, one who could be independent enough to feel comfortable with allowing someone to share her life, not run it—and last night Brandon had realized that he had found her.

Now he wondered just how he would be able to explain to her that he was not Paul, the man she had saved from committing suicide, but Brandon Michaels, an actor who had been rehearsing for a play. A type of rehearsal that he always did, and one that had labeled him as an eccentric.

Two years before, he had been the subject of an article in the *Daily News*, which had centered around his eccentricities. From the time he had learned that acting would be his career, Brandon had flung himself wholeheartedly into it. He had learned that when performing a part in a play, he had to live and think as the character he played. Most actors did this, but Brandon, a perfectionist, was never satisfied with his work, and had taken to rehearsing privately, almost becoming the characters he portrayed.

That was what had happened last night, when Lanie found him "attempting suicide." He was only rehearsing his lines, but actually being on the bridge gave him more of a feeling of reality and experience than two and a half months of rehearsals on the stage set. Nor, he thought, was last night the first time he had wandered onto the bridge. He had been going there twice weekly for almost a month.

Brandon opened his eyes and looked at his watch, seeing that it was almost midnight. Taking a deep breath, he reached for the telephone on the table next to him and picked up the receiver. After a few short rings, he was asking the hotel operator for Lanie's room.

The phone rang three times before it was answered, and the deep sound of a man's voice at the other end startled Brandon. Instead of hanging up, he asked for Lanie.

"I think you have the wrong room," said the man.

"Is this room eight-seven-three?" Brandon asked.

"You got that right," the stranger said.

"I—"

"Look friend, I just got in from Chicago, and I'd like to unpack and take a shower, if you don't mind."

"You just arrived? You just checked in?" Brandon asked.

"Ten minutes ago. Good-bye," the man snapped. Brandon heard the click of the phone, but his mind was still trying to absorb what had happened. His initial elation at discovering that the man was not a part of Lanie's life had quickly fled in the wake of his newfound knowledge that she was gone.

Moving as though he were caught in quicksand, he placed the receiver on its base and shook his head slowly. *What happened to her? Where was she?* Although he didn't want to admit it, he had no choice: She was gone. *But why?*

And, Brandon thought, she didn't even know his real name.

"Damn!" The word exploded from his lips with a savage anger that was completely different from his usual calmness, for he had realized that not only did she not know who he was, he hadn't the slightest idea who she was. He only knew her name was Lanie; he didn't know her last name at all.

Chapter 4

THE FIRST FAINT RAYS OF LIGHT EDGED SLOWLY OVER THE eastern horizon, chasing away the darkness of the night. Walking along the sandy beach, Elaine tried to ignore the coming day, for with the light the safety of the anonymity that had been hers for the past four months would be gone.

From the moment her plane had landed in Los Angeles four months ago, carrying her away from the fraud that Brandon Michaels had perpetrated upon her, until yesterday afternoon when she had left the studio, she had been able to submerge herself in her work and not think of him. Her days had been filled with hurried activity and intense concentration. Every minute of every working day had been utilized in the preproduction work necessary to have everything ready for the start of the filming of *Distant Worlds*.

And today would be the initial cast meeting of all the

actors appearing in *Distant Worlds*. Elaine's nerves were on edge, and she knew she would have to bring to bear every last ounce of her will to enable her to act normally and not show her true feelings to Brandon Michaels.

She wouldn't give him the satisfaction of letting him know that every night since she had left New York had passed with the slowness of an eternity. She refused to allow him to see how badly she had been hurt—*no, how much I still hurt,* she corrected herself.

Over the past months, Elaine had learned that honest self-perception was her true salvation. At first she had lied to herself, trying to convince herself that Brandon meant nothing at all, that their night together had been a mistake, meaningless. But the truth refused to be hidden and she finally faced it bravely. When she had done that, the intensity of her dreams had diminished slightly.

But no one must know, especially not Brandon, of the nights she woke calling his name, reaching for the man who wasn't there. Every morning, when Elaine woke, she chased away the dreams as best she could by walking along the sandy beach just as the sun rose in the sky. The walk was a catharsis of sorts, enabling her to clear her mind; and when she returned to her small house, she'd always found the strength to face the day.

But today things were different. She knew that she would have to face Brandon while maintaining her professional demeanor. Elaine prayed she would be able to—she knew she had to; her future and her career depended upon her self-control.

"You can do it, Lanie." Elaine stopped in her tracks and looked around, but no one was there. Then she realized that she had heard her father's voice in her mind.

These were the same words he had used two weeks ago when they had had dinner together one night. Turning back to her house, Lanie thought about that night, and the support and advice her father had given her.

Elaine had pulled her Datsun 260Z smoothly into the driveway of her father's Beverly Hills home. The car reacted as if it knew where it was, and Elaine believed it did. She was driving the same car her father had given her on her eighteenth birthday, and he'd given it to her here. Unlike so many of her friends, Elaine had felt no need to buy a new car when she'd finished school. She loved the small sports car and didn't need the pretentiousness of a newer, more expensive one.

The sight of the long driveway brought on a rush of memories. The neatly maintained lawn and trees reminded her of many happy times when she'd wanted nothing more in life than to play in her yard, secure under the watchful eyes of her parents.

Stopping the Datsun, Elaine had left the car and gone to the front door. She'd opened it and called out to her father.

"In here," he'd shouted from the kitchen.

When she entered the large kitchen, she'd found her father closing the oven door. She went to him and kissed him lightly on the cheek. "Smells delicious."

"It had better be!" he'd declared. "Dinner will be ready in a few minutes. Drink?" Lawrence Rodman had asked.

"Not now, Dad," Elaine had replied.

"In that case, why don't you open a bottle of Medoc, and I'll put dinner on the table."

"Fair enough," she'd replied.

Elaine found the bottle of wine sitting on the sideboard

in the dining room. She opened it carefully and placed it on the table to breathe for a few minutes. With that done, she had turned to look at the large oil painting of her mother that hung on the far wall of the room.

Annette Rodman had been a beautiful woman, with aristocratic good looks and a regal bearing. The portrait had been painted nine years ago, when Annette had turned forty-five. Her light hair had been streaked with gray, and Annette had refused to allow the artist to change the color to make her look younger.

Elaine nodded to herself at the memory. Her mother had been right, and the final product had been true to its living model. But five years after the portrait was painted, Elaine had lost her mother, who had always been her best friend.

Lawrence Rodman had been on location in Italy on one of his films and Annette had decided to fly over and surprise him. She had landed in Rome and then hired a private plane to fly her to the mountain region where the filming was being done. The plane encountered an unexpected storm over the mountains, and it was surmised that the engine malfunctioned, sending both the pilot and Annette Rodman to their deaths.

It took a long time for Lawrence and Elaine to recover, and it was only the ability to share their grief and loss that had made life bearable for them. In time their wounds had healed, but neither of them ever forgot Annette, and their love for her stayed strong.

"Ready?" Lawrence had asked as he carried the large serving platter to the table.

"Always. Dad, do you still miss her?" Elaine had asked suddenly.

When Lawrence Rodman turned to face his daughter, Elaine had seen the answer in his eyes. "Lanie, there isn't a day that passes that I don't think of her and miss her. Sometimes I . . ."

Elaine had crossed the distance between them and gone into her father's arms. "I'm sorry," she'd whispered.

"For what? For asking me an important question? Lanie, we both loved her very, very much."

They'd held each other for a few moments, and then her father had gently eased her away. "Besides," he'd said with a smile, "I spent an hour in the kitchen, and dinner is about to get cold."

"Yes, sir!" Elaine had said with an exaggerated salute. She poured the wine and then sat at the place that had been set for her. While they ate, their conversation had been light, and her father had barely touched on the various aspects of her work. After dinner, and after Elaine had insisted on making the coffee and serving it in the den, her father's questions had begun to delve deeper into what she was doing.

"I spoke to David last week," he'd begun, "and he tells me that you're doing an excellent job."

"I'm doing whatever I'm allowed to," Elaine had answered dryly.

"Allowed to?"

"C'mon Dad, *Distant Worlds* is David's project. I feel that I'm a figurehead and not much more."

"Why?" Lawrence asked.

"I don't seem to have much say in the movie."

"That's not my understanding. I thought you were the movie's producer."

Elaine had stared at her father for a moment and then she'd shaken her head slowly. Standing, she'd walked to the shelf that held her father's three Oscars and studied them before turning to reply.

"David Leaser told me that this film is his pet project. The casting was done before I was given the film. He made it clear, in no uncertain terms, that it would stay just the way it was."

"You replaced the original producer, you inherited the cast, but that doesn't mean you aren't the producer."

"I disagree with the casting of the lead actor."

"Brandon Michaels? Why?"

Elaine hadn't been able to meet her father's eyes, and had turned to face the three golden images. "I don't think he's right for the part."

"But the casting department and Trion Studios do think he's right, and that bothers you?"

"Yes. This is my first movie as a producer, and I want it to be a good one," she'd said, turning to face her father again.

"Then I suggest you make it a good one, and if this actor doesn't do the job you feel he should, then it's up to you and the director to make sure he does."

"Dad . . ."

"No! You were the one who wanted to be a producer. You were the one who came to me and told me that you had decided what you wanted to do with your life. Now that you've been given the chance, you're trying to tell me that it's unfair, that you're being held back?"

Elaine had recoiled from the ferocity in her father's voice. It was only rarely that she saw him angry, and if she had never liked it when his anger had been directed at another, she hated it now when it was pointed at her. "No, that's not it," she'd said defensively.

"Then what is it? Lanie, you've proven yourself

capable of being a producer; that's why David gave you this picture. Instead of trying to show the world how great you are, do the best job you can and let your work speak for you."

Elaine had gazed at her father, hesitantly nodding her head. He was right, and his advice was correct, given the knowledge he had. Elaine could not bring herself to tell him the real reason for her doubts about producing the movie.

"Good, then please do me a favor."

"What?"

"You already know how proud of you I am. Now, no matter what problems you encounter, deal with them and make yourself just as proud. Lanie, you can do it!"

Elaine had blinked back the sudden mist that veiled her eyes. "I will," she'd promised him.

"I will," she told the leading edge of the sun when it finally rose in the sky. Taking a deep breath of the cool morning air, Elaine walked purposefully toward her house, her stomach rumbling an echo to her words.

An hour later, Elaine was sitting at her desk, sipping coffee and going over the notes her assistant had left on her desk the night before. She'd signed one acquisition request and was about to approve another when her intercom buzzed.

"Yes?" she asked.

"Mr. Hart would like to see you," Bonnie Walsh, her secretary, informed her.

"Send him in." Elaine clicked off the intercom and took a deep breath. *What now?*

An uneasy truce had been declared between her and her director, John Hart. Hart had not been happy when Elaine took over the reins from Tom Sellert; the two men had been friends for a long time. But Hart knew that Elaine had been handpicked by David Leaser, and that there could be no arguments—his only recourse would be to quit the picture. John Hart had not yet attained the status where he could let his opinions rule him and still survive in the business.

Elaine glanced up just as the director came in, leaving the door ajar. She nodded at the chair across from her desk and watched him move toward it. John Hart was about five-foot-eight and thin framed, with small, delicate hands —the type of hands people called artistic. His face was handsome enough, and his gray eyes were alive with movement. His hair was dark and curly and his full beard seemed to be an extension of a creative facade. Hart was a good director, and although Elaine knew he resented her, she was glad he was on the project.

Elaine took another sip of coffee, waiting for Hart to speak. The moment her cup reached the table, John Hart began.

"Have you heard from Michaels yet?" he asked.

"No," Elaine replied, certain that her self-control was in check.

"Well, no one else has either. He finished the play two weeks ago, and he's disappeared."

" 'Disappeared'?" Elaine asked, raising her eyebrows slightly and exerting full control over her emotions.

"That's what I said," Hart replied sarcastically.

"I would think that he hasn't disappeared officially until the start of the cast meeting."

"Look, I called his agent last night to make sure he'd gotten the last changes in the script. His agent said he didn't know if Michaels had or not because he hadn't spoken to him since before he left the play.''

"So?"

"So," Hart echoed as he shook his head, "I'm worried that he'll hold up production.''

"That's my worry, not yours," Elaine advised him.

"Look, Miss Rodman, this entire film is my worry.''

"It's mine also! We share a common bond, don't we?" she asked in a honey-sweet voice.

"No, we don't. This picture can make me or it can break me, but you have your father to call if you get into trouble.''

A sudden surge of anger surprised her and before she could dampen it, she lashed out. "My father has nothing to do with this movie or my career. If you can't accept that, and if you can't accept that I, not my father, am the producer of this movie, then I suggest you get off the picture and out of my office!''

"Just who the he—''

Before he could finish, Elaine cut him off. "Elaine Rodman, the producer of this movie, is who the *hell* I am, and I think you had best remember that. Is there anything else you wish to discuss?" Elaine asked as she fought to control her rage.

John Hart stood—almost leapt—from the chair, his face scarlet. "Well, Miss Producer, I hope your star shows up today and—''

Once again Elaine cut him off before he went too far. "Brandon Michaels will show up, Mr. Director, and just make sure you're prepared to do your job. Now, if there's nothing else . . .''

Hart stared at her for a moment before he turned and marched stiffly from the office. When the door snapped shut, Elaine breathed a sigh of relief. "What a way to start a film," she said to her coffee mug.

But the director's words had bothered her; not his innuendos about her father, but his words about Brandon Michaels. Elaine had risen to his defense unthinkingly, but she intuitively knew that no matter what her feelings were about him, he was a serious and dedicated actor, and he would be here. She wondered if she should call his agent, but decided to wait and see what happened.

She looked for her attaché case and realized that it wasn't by her desk. She pressed the intercom and asked Bonnie if it was in the outer office, and her secretary told her no. Shrugging her shoulders, Elaine rose, thinking she'd probably left it in the car, and set out for the parking lot.

The sun's splendor shone with a magnificent power, accenting the sapphire blue of the Pacific Ocean, making each small wave sparkle with the luminescence of a jewel. For Brandon Michaels, the view from the redwood deck of the Topanga Beach house was almost as spectacular as the view from his penthouse window in New York.

He had been here for almost ten days, and had enjoyed the relative peace and quiet of the large beach house belonging to Mi-Tech, his computer consulting firm. He had made arrangements, when he'd signed the contract for *Distant Worlds*, to have the house prepared for him.

Originally he'd chosen this site for its convenience to Los Angeles and for its low-key ambience. It was a stone's throw north of Malibu, but not as well known or as popular as the other beach community. Topanga Beach offered him the solitude and quiet he needed to get in to his role for the upcoming filming.

And he had thrown himself into his new part, eschewing any contact with the outside world until today, when he would go to Trion Studios to meet the cast and crew for the first time.

Closing his eyes for a moment, he used his photographic memory to recall Lanie's face. He had done this same thing every morning since she'd left New York. He knew he was being foolish, but he refused to give up his need to remember her as he had last seen her, peacefully asleep, her face glowing softly in the morning sun just before he had closed the curtains.

Brandon had tried to forget her, putting all his considerable determination into the effort, but when each day dawned, he found himself wanting only to see her, to hold her. For the first time in his life, Brandon Michaels was unable to get what he wanted, and nothing he had been able to do had changed that.

Brandon laughed ruefully. He had even tried to get her name from the hotel clerk, only to be stiffly informed that the guest in room 873 had left specific instructions that no information about her be given out.

That in itself had not stopped Brandon from trying, but not knowing her last name and her not being from New York had made it impossible to locate her. *Perhaps I'll find her here,* he thought, remembering that Lanie was from California. But Brandon knew that California was a big, big state.

The honking of a car horn brought him back to the present. Picking up the script and the memo attached to it, he left the deck by the side steps, waving to the driver of the car that had just arrived.

"Good morning, superstar!" Simon Arnold shouted in a cheerful greeting.

"And to you, oh great scribe," Brandon joked in return

as he opened the door and got into the passenger seat of the Mercedes 450 SL convertible sports coupé.

"Like it?" Simon asked as he waved his hand to encompass the car.

"Beautiful. Trying to get into the swing of L.A.?"

"I've always wanted a Mercedes, and now I can afford it."

"As long as you wanted it for yourself, and not to be a part of Hollywood."

"You hurt me to the bone," Simon said, his voice filled with simulated pain.

"I don't, but the fast crowd will," Brandon said seriously.

"Only if I let them. Ease up, Bran, everyone knows what you think of the movie industry, but it does pay the bills, and you might even like it once you get going," he advised.

Before Brandon could reply, Simon put the car into gear and backed out of the driveway. After he negotiated the various turns, he guided the car onto U.S. 1, and headed toward Los Angeles. "Be there in about a half hour," he told Brandon.

"That may be too soon," Brandon said dryly. Then he sat back and watched the road, letting his mind roam.

A short time later, Brandon turned to Simon with another question. "Tell me about them," he asked as they crossed into Los Angeles.

" 'Them'?"

"Simon . . ." Brandon's tone made Simon smile. Then he nodded and began to speak.

"They all seem very professional. John Hart is the director, which you know, and he seems a nice enough guy."

Brandon glanced at Simon for a moment. He caught a strange inflection in his friend's voice. "But?" he prompted.

"He's all right, just a little taken with his own abilities, but most directors are."

"What did he want to change in the script?" Brandon asked wisely.

"Nothing major, he was just trying to see how far I would bend."

"How far did you?"

"Not at all!"

"Good. What about the producer?" Brandon asked. He had seen the woman's name on several memos sent to him, and had thought she'd presented a very businesslike and efficient front, at least on paper.

"I've met Elaine Rodman several times, and she seems to be very capable and thorough. I was surprised, after what I'd heard about her."

"And what was that?" Brandon asked, wishing that Simon would just get to the point instead of having to have every last detail pulled from his mouth. But after five years of knowing him, Brandon was used to the playwright's ways.

"She's Lawrence Rodman's daughter."

"So?"

"The rumors have it that he used his influence to get her the job."

"You just said she seemed capable."

"I did, but who knows. If she's a producer's brat, we'll all know soon enough. Here we are," Simon said, turning off the freeway and onto a side street.

Brandon sat back and watched as Trion Studios came

into view. When Simon stopped the car at the gate, Brandon extended the pass that was attached to the script.

The guard examined both their passes and then nodded his head. "Welcome to Trion, Mr. Michaels. Mr. Arnold, please use Lot Three, to your left."

Simon drove into the designated parking lot. While he looked for a spot, Brandon studied the studio buildings. Then his eyes caught a movement to his left, and he froze.

Not believing his eyes, he watched a woman who could be Lanie's twin sister close the door on a Datsun 260 Z and begin to walk toward a building. "Stop!" he ordered.

"I have to find a space first," Simon said.

"Dammit, stop the car!" Before the words were all out, Brandon had opened the door and jumped from the moving vehicle. He landed smoothly and began to run after the woman. He saw her enter a doorway and redoubled his efforts to catch her. From the shape of her back and her height, he knew it had to be Lanie.

A bare three seconds after she'd disappeared behind the door, Brandon was through it. He saw her turn a corner down the hall, and he was off again. When he rounded the corner, he saw an office door close, and went directly to it. Without bothering to read the lettering on the glass, he opened the door and barged in.

Brandon froze again when his eyes met those of the woman who was seated behind the desk.

"Can I help you?" she asked.

Brandon took several breaths to try and ease the racing of his pulse, caused in part by his running and in part by seeing Lanie.

"A woman just came in here . . ."

"You're very observant," Bonnie said quickly.

"I need to see her," Brandon stated, ignoring the girl's remark.

"Do you have an appointment?" she asked.

"An appointment?" Brandon shook his head slowly. "I just want to see Lanie."

"I'm sorry, but Miss Rodman is very busy."

"Miss Rodman? Lanie Rodman?"

"Elaine Rodman, yes," Bonnie said with a nod of her head.

Suddenly everything fell into place. The weeks and months of wondering why she had disappeared from his life had been solved. It happened so quickly that Brandon couldn't stop a foolish smile from spreading across his face. He didn't hear the secretary speak until she had repeated herself.

"Would you please tell me what you want?" Bonnie asked again.

"Miss Rodman is working on *Distant Worlds*, isn't she?"

"Yes. Now if you'll state your business, I can set up an appointment with her for you."

Brandon couldn't stop smiling, and he didn't care what the secretary thought of him. "Please tell Miss Rodman that Brandon Michaels would like to speak to her."

"Just a moment," Bonnie said, after she had digested this information. She was about to press the intercom, but changed her mind. She'd overheard the argument between the director and Elaine through the slightly open door, and decided that she should announce the movie's star herself. She thought Elaine might like that, and Bonnie was secretly glad that Elaine wouldn't suffer because the actor hadn't shown up on schedule.

Rising from her chair, Bonnie went to the door, knocked lightly and then slipped inside, to find Elaine gazing at her quizzically.

"Is something wrong?" Elaine asked.

"No, it's right. You'll be able to show John Hart up. Brandon Michaels is here."

"Here? As in on the lot?" she asked, her stomach churning.

"No, here, as in on the other side of your door."

"Oh, no," Elaine whispered. *I'm not ready*, she thought. Taking a deep breath, she smiled tentatively at Bonnie. "Tell Mr. Michaels that I'll see him on the sound stage in ten minutes with the rest of the cast."

"Miss Rodman, I—"

"Please do as I ask," Elaine said.

"Very well," Bonnie replied. A moment later, the door closed quietly behind Bonnie. Elaine took several rapid breaths as she tried to regain her badly upset equilibrium. The inevitable had happened, and she hadn't been ready for it.

But now she knew she must take the next few minutes to rebuild her composure and prepare herself for facing Brandon Michaels.

In the outer office, Bonnie hesitantly told Brandon what Elaine had said. When she finished, she sat down, avoiding his eyes.

Brandon kept his smile in place, even when he heard Elaine's message. Instead of just crashing through the door to face her, he turned and silently left. He had to think, needing a few minutes to try and understand.

The only thing he was certain of was that Elaine Rodman and Lanie, the woman who had "saved his life," were one and the same.

He realized what must have happened in New York. Lanie had left a message that she was going to the theater. What she hadn't said was which one. Now Brandon knew. She had seen *Lifelines,* and had learned just who "Paul" was.

"Stupid!" he berated himself.

"Bran," called Simon Arnold.

Brandon looked up and saw Simon walking toward him with an attractive blonde at his side. He recognized her immediately, and extended his hand. "I'm glad to meet you, Miss Reed," he said, taking her hand in a firm grip and shaking it. Brandon had spoken truthfully; he had been looking forward to working with Cynthia Reed. She was an excellent actress, and from what he knew of her, didn't seem to be one of the "Hollywood" types.

"The pleasure is mine," she replied. "I've been looking forward to meeting and working with you," Cynthia said as she released his hand.

"I guess I don't have to introduce you, then, do I? Brandon, what happened to you?" Simon asked.

"I saw her," he said.

"Her?" Simon repeated, then he nodded. "The woman from the bridge?"

"I saw her, but I couldn't get to see her."

"I think you've lost me," Cynthia said.

"He has that habit," Simon joked, but noting the expression on his friend's face, he quickly changed the subject. "But that's another story, and if we don't get a move on, we'll miss the meeting."

Sensing that what had been said was private, Cynthia inclined her head and began to walk toward the sound stage with the two men, but she couldn't help wondering what Simon had meant, and hoped that she could find out about it later. No, she hoped she would have the opportunity to see Simon later, she admitted to herself. Cynthia had met the playwright at a party three weeks ago, and had found herself very attracted to the tall, slender man. From the moment she'd first spoken to him she'd wanted him to ask her out.

Just as they reached the sound stage for *Distant Worlds,* Cynthia paused. "We made it in time. Here comes Lanie," she said, pointing to the oncoming figure of Elaine Rodman.

"Lanie?" both Simon and Brandon said in unison.

"Elaine Rodman, our producer."

"You know her?" Simon asked quickly, his eyes flicking from Brandon to Cynthia.

"Of course I do, we grew up together. . . . Why?" she asked.

"Later," Simon said quickly.

"Tonight?" Cynthia asked him without batting an eyelash. Cynthia was, if nothing else, a pragmatist.

Simon smiled warmly. "Tonight."

Both of them turned to look at Brandon, but in the short amount of time it had taken them to make the date, he had slipped inside the sound stage door.

"Simon?" Cynthia asked.

"Later, I promise."

"Hi, Cindy, Mr. Arnold," Elaine said with a tight smile.

"Hi, Lanie, ready to start?" she asked.

"I see you already have," Elaine snapped tartly.

"Lanie!" Cynthia called to her back.

Cynthia gazed up at Simon, and then shrugged her shoulders.

"It's a long story. I'll tell you later."

"And a good one, I hope," she said as she slipped her arm through Simon's, and they followed Elaine inside.

Chapter 5

THE NIGHT WAS CHILLY, AND THE BREEZE BLOWING IN from the Pacific only added to the coolness, which helped fuel Elaine's mood. She was sitting on the floor in the living room, dressed in old, faded jeans and a light sweater, letting the warmth from the fire she had built ease her tension.

The day that had just ended had been a long, hard one, and had drained her both physically and emotionally. First the argument with John Hart, then Brandon's surprise visit to her office, and finally the cast-and-crew meeting, which had lasted for four and a half hours.

Whenever she had spoken, she'd been acutely aware of Brandon's green eyes locked on her face. Whenever she walked around or spoke to anyone, she sensed Brandon staring at her, and when she had turned, she'd found she'd been right. At one point she'd had a flashing memory of that long-ago night, and had again felt his strong, tender hands roaming along the length of her body. She'd almost screamed out in her struggle to banish those feelings and thoughts from her mind and to focus her attention on the people surrounding her.

After all the business had been taken care of Elaine had introduced the production crew, and then turned the meeting over to John Hart, who introduced the cast to everyone. When the shooting schedule was announced and the locations explained, the meeting broke into small groups so that everyone could get to know one another better.

At the end of the meeting Elaine had once again risen to speak, announcing that rehearsals would begin tomorrow morning at seven, and that the crew was expected to be there also, although they wouldn't be shooting yet. The cast, however, she had informed them, would be expected in their dressing rooms by six-thirty, during the three days of rehearsal, and at five-thirty for makeup and costuming when the filming commenced. This was met with mixed groans.

The meeting had ended then, and as Elaine had walked toward the exit, she'd seen Brandon break away from a small group and begin to follow her. Elaine had slipped into the hallway, and then into the ladies' room. She'd waited for ten minutes before venturing out. The hallway had been clear, and she'd gone to her office. Perhaps, she'd hoped, Brandon had gotten the message.

As she watched the licking orange-and-yellow flames, Elaine realized how childish she had acted today. Hiding from Brandon was not a solution, and Elaine knew that she must face him soon. She also knew that she needed to face him on her own terms, at a time of her own choosing.

Her lack of control of the situation was what had upset her today.

Tomorrow, she promised herself, and Elaine's promises to herself were not taken lightly. She would seek him out tomorrow at a propitious moment and try to make him understand that she wanted the past to remain there, and not affect the picture, or either of their careers.

How could I still be in love with him? How could I have fallen in love in just one night? Elaine asked herself again. Those two questions had plagued her for four months, and she still had no answer. The only thing she knew with any certainty concerning herself and Brandon Michaels was that she had fallen hopelessly in love with him. Sighing, Elaine stared deep into the fire, trying to erase the memory of that long-ago night, and to banish the haunting memories that still followed her, no matter how hard she tried to deny her love.

"Are you sure you didn't make that up to impress me with your wit?" Cynthia Reed asked.

"It does seem rather fictional, doesn't it?" Simon replied with a slow grin. "Remember, you promised not to mention a word."

"I'll remember," Cindy said as she lifted her coffee cup and took a sip. "At least that explains why Elaine has been acting so strangely lately."

"Not to mention Brandon," Simon added. Then he sat back and glanced around the restaurant. La Cuisine was a small, romantic restaurant that overlooked the Pacific. It was not a well-known restaurant frequented by vast crowds, which was the reason Simon had picked it for their first date.

"I still can't believe it. It's so unlike Elaine," Cindy said in a hushed tone.

"But not unlike Brandon."

"He does that sort of thing often? Uses his stage name to seduce women?" Cindy asked in a tight voice. She had liked Brandon when she'd talked with him, and had looked forward to working with him, but Elaine was her closest friend, and if Brandon had hurt her, she wouldn't take kindly to it. Simon's laugh caught Cindy off guard, and she raised her eyebrows in question.

"No, that's not what I meant. Brandon really puts himself into the role he plays. He doesn't use it for convenience. What I meant was that Brandon is a very serious man. He doesn't play games, and he doesn't hurt people. When he met Elaine, something happened to him, Cynthia. He hasn't been the same since the opening night of *Lifelines*."

"Do you think he fell in love with her?"

"I wouldn't put it past him."

"That's a strange way to say yes."

"Cynthia, I'm not a run-of-the-mill person." Simon said it lightly, but his eyes locked with Cindy's, and they stayed that way for several long moments. "But," he said finally, "you have to get up early, and look as beautiful as you do tonight."

"Thank you," Cindy said. A wave of unexpected pleasure raced through her at his words, and she sensed he had not spoken playfully.

Simon called for the check, and then they left the restaurant and he drove Cindy home. At her front door, he hesitantly kissed her good night.

Then, with a smile on his face, he drove to the house he had rented for the duration of the filming. But Simon saw neither the road nor the night; rather, he saw visions of Cynthia Reed dancing before his eyes.

Although he had spoken of Brandon's seriousness when it came to women, he hadn't told her of his own. One of the reasons he and Brandon had become such close friends was that they shared similar outlooks on life. Like Brandon, Simon disliked the frivolous women who were associated with the entertainment industry. Like Brandon, Simon did not date often, and very rarely saw the same women more than a few times.

But tonight, after spending three hours with Cynthia Reed, he'd discovered she was not only an attractive woman, but a smart, sensitive and strong person as well.

Humming a tune to himself, Simon pulled into the driveway in a peaceful, happy frame of mind.

The clock on the living-room wall chimed the hour. Elaine stood and stretched, knowing that she should go to bed; she would have to be up and ready for work in just a few hours.

The fire was almost out, and the few glowing coals that remained would go out by themselves in a little while, so all she did was make sure the glass screen was in place so that no sparks could escape.

Elaine went into the kitchen, hung up the phone receiver, which she'd placed on the counter so that she wouldn't be disturbed tonight and shut off the light. Before she reached her bedroom, the doorbell rang.

Elaine stopped in her tracks, wondering who would have the nerve to visit her at this hour. Shrugging her shoulders, she went to the front door and opened it. The instant she had, she regretted the act. Standing before her, framed by the light of the hallway, was Brandon Michaels. Elaine's mind reeled, and her breathing stopped. She fought the wave of emotion that attacked her and forced her paralyzed vocal chords to work.

"I thought I made it plain enough that I didn't want to see you," she finally managed to say.

"Very, but we do have to work together," he stated.

"And we will, but that's all we'll do," she snapped in a stiff voice.

"Elaine, please let me come inside."

"Why?" she asked bluntly.

"Because we have to talk. Because you deserve an explanation."

"I deserved an explanation four months ago, on a night that I think best forgotten."

"And I think you're wrong. If you had stayed you would have received your explanation. If you hadn't run away from me."

"I flew, as a matter of fact."

"Please, Elaine."

The power of his green eyes assaulted her. The soft resonance of his voice was like a long-awaited caress, and the barriers Elaine had carefully erected were slowly crumbling. She knew she might be making a mistake, but something in his gaze made her resolve weaken.

"Why, Brandon?" she whispered as she stepped back.

Brandon entered the house and followed her into the warm living room. By the time he'd reached a chair, he had taken in the room and silently applauded Elaine's taste.

The living room was decorated simply, which gave it an air of elegance. The luminescence of the ebbing fire added its own warmth.

"It's lovely," he told her.

Elaine nodded, and then sat on the couch across from him. "You said you wanted to explain?" she prompted.

"I'm sorry I hurt you—"

"What makes you think that?" Elaine sniped, interrupting his apology. "Your ego?"

"My heart," he whispered.

Elaine's sharp intake of breath was loud in the room, against the crackling of the banked fire. She tried to control herself, but that seemed to be impossible. Instead, she willed herself to silence.

Brandon gazed at Elaine, ignoring the rancor in her voice and, for the moment, simply enjoying her beauty. It had been four long months, and he wouldn't give this moment up for anything.

"When I left your hotel room that morning I found myself wanting to stay, but I couldn't. I left the rose in my place. Then I went to the theater, because it was opening night and there were a thousand things to be done.

"But I went home the minute the curtain came down, and listened to my machine. I waited until midnight, and then I called you. The first thing I intended to tell you was my real name. I was going to tell you the truth, and explain what I was doing on the bridge."

"Playing a game," Elaine snapped.

"Please let me finish," Brandon pleaded in a low voice. He waited a moment, and when Elaine remained silent, he continued as if there had been no interruption.

"I've been called eccentric by a lot of people, and perhaps I am, but I do the very best job I can to make people believe me when I'm onstage. I was on the bridge because I needed to understand the feelings of my character. I needed to feel the wind, to almost taste what it would be like to fall to the water beneath me. I can imagine a lot of things, but not what it would be like to try to kill myself. That emotion is totally foreign to me.''

Elaine gazed at him, and at the soft shadows made by the dying fire. She saw the honesty in his eyes, and could see the control he was exercising in the tightness of his features. *Be careful!* she warned herself.

''But after you came down, after we were in the hotel . . .''

''I tried to tell you, but you wouldn't listen to me.''

''You what?'' Taken completely off guard, Elaine shouted the words.

''Think back, think about being on the bridge and think about the hotel. I tried to explain, but you stopped me. You couldn't have known I was trying to tell you I was an actor. I'm sure you thought I was going to explain my reasons for committing suicide, and you stopped me. You said 'Leave what happened in the past; it's where it belongs.' ''

''Because I believed that, just as I believed you wouldn't try to kill yourself again. I was a good audience, wasn't I?''

''Elaine—Lanie, you did something on the bridge that very few people would. You gave of yourself, for someone else. It affected me strongly.''

''Strongly enough for you to seduce me?'' Elaine asked suddenly, almost, but not quite, regretting the rashness of her comment.

''I came back to your room because I couldn't walk out of your life. Because I wanted to explain myself to you.''

Elaine continued to stare at him, but the swelling tide of her emotions was rising fast and she was afraid that she would give in. His words sounded truthful, and her heart responded to everything he said. Her heart cried out for

him, but she was afraid to let him know, afraid to trust
him with what she was feeling.

"I've spent the last four months looking for you.
Whenever I walked down the street I looked for you. I
tried to bribe the hotel clerk, but that didn't work."

Elaine started to speak, but the words refused to come.
She swallowed, and then took a deep breath. There was
something she had to know. "Why did you try to find
me?" she whispered hoarsely.

"Because I fell in love with you."

A bomb couldn't have made a louder explosion in her
mind than his words. Her entire body was rocked by his
admission, and she fought vainly to calm herself.

"Brandon, it was only one night."

"Where is it written that it takes more than that to
know?" he demanded in a suddenly loud voice.

"I . . ."

"Elaine, we've wasted four months. Let's not waste
any more time."

Elaine fought her battle and won some degree of
composure. Sitting up straighter on the couch, she shook
her head slowly. "It won't work," she told him, but
couldn't quite meet his open stare.

"Look at me and say that again."

Elaine couldn't. "Please, Brandon, don't do this to
me."

"If what happened between us in New York meant
nothing to you, you wouldn't have left! You wouldn't have
turned me away in your office today, and you wouldn't
have left the meeting and disappeared!"

"Perhaps I'm just eccentric," she ventured.

"No, but you are beautiful," he whispered.

"Brandon . . ."

"I've told you the truth. Do you believe me?" he asked.

Elaine was caught unprepared for his question, and she gazed at him for a long moment before she nodded her head. "I believe you . . ."

"But?"

"But what I said that night must be said again. Leave the past where it belongs, Brandon. We're working together, but that's all."

"No. Elaine, you can think whatever you want to about me, but I love you, and I believe you love me, too."

"Is that your ego talking?" she asked, shocked that he could know how she felt about him.

"No, it's reality. That night when we made love it was because something happened between us. It was no one-night stand, not strangers passing. What happened to us was real and, dammit, you know that as well as I!"

Elaine closed her eyes to deny his words, but the truth remained in her mind. He was right, but she wouldn't give in, she mustn't—she already knew the dangers of doing that.

Brandon looked at Elaine, feeling helpless to do anything. He wanted to convince her, to prove his words to be the truth. "Lanie—"

"Don't," she cried, interrupting whatever it was that he had been about to say. "Please leave me alone."

Brandon rose suddenly, towering over Elaine. Yet she sat stiffly, unable to move.

"All right, Elaine. I don't know what else to say to you to convince you that I'm telling the truth. I'll see you tomorrow." With that, Brandon turned and left the living room.

Elaine watched him walk away, and felt herself turn to

ice. For the second time since she met him, he was about to walk out on her. Then the iciness that had gripped her was shattered by the scorching intensity of her rage. She stood quickly, her chest rising and falling rapidly.

"Bravo!" she shouted, clapping her hands. "Well done! Brandon Michaels has won his audience again."

Brandon stopped, his back stiffening as her words tore through him. Slowly, with his fists balled against his sides, he turned to face her.

"Is that what you think?" he asked in a forceful voice, his eyes hard and piercing.

Elaine didn't flinch from the anger radiating from him; instead, she drew her shoulders straighter. "What else am I supposed to think? You come in here and tell me a fairy tale about falling in love with me, yet you couldn't even tell me your real name after we had made love. Dammit, Brandon, you're a hell of an actor. You convinced me in New York and you almost did it again tonight!"

"Almost doesn't count," Brandon whispered.

"It's as close as I care to get," Elaine retorted.

Brandon heard her words but refused to let them stop him. He shook his head, and threw all caution away. He reached her in four long strides and, before she could react, caught her in his arms, crushing her against him, his mouth covering hers almost bruisingly in its intensity.

Elaine had seen his face change, but before she could raise her arms to ward him off, he was on her. His arms encircled her, and the steel bands they'd become afforded her no release. She drew her head back from his descending lips, but to no avail, as his hot mouth covered hers, burning and bruising.

She tried to twist her torso away, but the power in his arms prevented even that. Then, like a lightning bolt striking her, a fiery, searing blaze leaped upward, destroying all her resistance. The heat of his body was like a fire leaping through her body, and the more she struggled, the more powerful the sensations became.

She sagged against him, half in dismay, half in shocked surprise at the treasonous way her body was reacting. Then his mouth softened, and she became all too aware of the sweetness of his lips.

Her blood pounded in her ears and her lungs were threatening to explode by the time Brandon pulled his mouth from hers.

She opened her eyes and stared into the mysterious, blazing depths of his. She was afraid to speak, afraid to even whisper for fear he would hear how badly the kiss had affected her. She shook her head in a denial of what her body was demanding; her tension and dismay combined to make tears spring to her eyes. Once again she tried to pull out of his grasp.

Ignoring the molten heat of his blood, Brandon gazed at her. The twin paths of her silent tears sparkled in the low light of the room. Suddenly he realized what he had done. "I'm sorry, Elaine," he whispered.

"So am I," she replied in a halting voice.

Elaine stared at him for a moment, caught within the electric tension swirling in the air. With everything that had happened tonight, she was afraid of what might follow.

Brandon lowered his mouth toward hers again. "No," she whispered, closing her eyes against the apparition that haunted her. "Please."

Suddenly, the bands of iron that had been imprisoning her were gone and she was free. Opening her eyes slowly, she saw Brandon's tension-lined face.

"Brandon," she began, doing her best to keep her voice level. "We can't . . . We both made a mistake in New York, and I can't allow myself to repeat it. We have five months ahead of us that we have to spend together. It has to be as professionals."

"We can't deny our emotions," he told her.

"I have to deny mine." Elaine turned from him, walked to the fireplace and stared into the ashes of the fire. "This film is very important to me. I've worked for four years to earn the right to produce it. There are a lot of people at Trion who want to see me fall on my face. I . . . I won't let that happen."

"Are you telling me that your career is the most important thing to you?" Brandon asked as he studied her back. He yearned to go to her, to hold her against him, not in the wild passion that had been unleashed moments before, but in a gentle and secure embrace.

"It is important, but . . ." she said, wondering how he could even think such a thing.

"But nothing!" he snapped angrily. "I think you should get your priorities in order!"

Elaine whirled to face him, her rage rising once again. "And I suppose you think you should be my most important priority?" she retaliated.

"Don't you?" he whispered.

Elaine stopped herself from rising to the bait and took a deep, calming breath. "As I was saying, we have to work together. This is your first film, and mine as well, in a manner of speaking. Let's not fight our way through it."

"You know you're in love with me, don't you?" Brandon asked, purposely ignoring what Elaine had just said.

His words echoed madly in her mind, and she fought

against the hypnotic effect of his eyes until she was able to breathe again.

"The only thing I'm aware of is that you're a wonderful actor who, sadly, shares the same proclivity toward dramatics and egocentricity as do most of your breed."

"You're only speaking words, Lanie. You're not talking from your heart. I *know* how you feel."

"Brandon, you have rehearsal in a few hours. Please go home and get some rest."

"You see, you do care!" Brandon declared with an infuriating smile.

"Good night, Brandon," she said.

"I won't give you up, Lanie."

The intense stare he favored her with made her shiver. It also made her believe him. "Brandon, let's work together as friends."

"We never were friends, Lanie. We started out being much more than that. Good night, Elaine. I'll see you tomorrow."

Before Elaine could react he was gone. She called out his name, but the closing of the front door drowned out her barely audible whisper. All that remained was the haunting image of the insolent smile he had flashed before he'd turned and walked out into the night.

She shivered as her blood began to race through her veins. She had known, while she was denying his words to his face, that he had read her heart, and had spoken only the truth as he saw it. But she couldn't tell him that she loved him. She couldn't admit that to the only person who would be able to use that knowledge to his own benefit. She loved him, but she didn't trust him. And that was as important to love as was the love itself.

Her mind was filled with a chaotic mass of thoughts,

with every word that Brandon had uttered tonight swirling madly within it. *Have I made another mistake?* she wondered, as the memory of his burning kiss gripped her in a tight hold. He'd told her he loved her. She had seen the truth in his eyes; but she had been too afraid to believe it.

Yet the very thing she feared most surfaced in her mind—her own goals and ambitions were on the block. She was being tested right now, and it was a trial by fire. If she were to be a success, she had to start with this film. Could she do that and also maintain a relationship with a man who seemed so ill-equipped to handle the responsibility of a real relationship? She didn't know the answer, and not knowing was another reason for her fear.

Elaine sank onto the rug in front of the fireplace and stared at the ashes without seeing them. Her mind was almost blank as her emotions continued to do battle.

"That's good, keep it coming," shouted John Hart to the five actors standing in the center of the sound stage.

Elaine stood next to one of the idle cameras, watching the proceedings. It was nearing noon, and the first rehearsal was in full swing. She had been on the set since early morning, ignoring her paperwork because she wanted to make sure that everything got off to a good start. And, she admitted to herself, to make sure she could watch Brandon work without revealing the emotions that were so much a part of her. Just seeing him and hearing his powerful voice was enough to bring back the memory of last night's burning kiss. *Stop!* she ordered herself, and turned her thoughts to the director.

Unlike many directors, John Hart believed in holding a minimum of rehearsals, preferring instead to let the actors have just a small period of time to familiarize themselves with their characters. He believed that if the actors were professionals, they would have the part down before reporting to work.

In that, Elaine agreed with him. And she saw that everyone, from Brandon and Cynthia to the bit players, had indeed learned their lines before setting foot on the rehearsal stage. Hart's three days of rehearsals would serve to convey to the actors Hart's interpretation of the screenplay.

"I see things are moving along quite well," came a familiar voice.

Elaine turned to find herself face to face with Thomas Sellert, the film's ex-producer. "It's going well enough," Elaine replied stiffly.

"Why did you do it?" Sellert asked in a low, intense voice.

"Do what?"

"Use your father's influence to get me kicked off the movie and yourself put on?"

Elaine flushed, but refused to give in to him. "I did no such thing!"

"The hell you didn't. I've watched the way you've moved up the ladder over the men who were in your way. Better people than you, better producer material, but you had your father behind you. All they had was themselves. And then you did it to me!"

"You did it to yourself," Elaine said quietly. "It was you, not I, who lost you *Distant Worlds!*"

"One day I'll get even with you," he threatened.

"Sellert, the film is my project, and this is a restricted area. You have no authority, or pass, to be here, so please leave, now!"

"You like having power, don't you?"

Rather than answer him and risk being drawn deeper into a pointless argument, Elaine ignored his last comment and glanced around. Walking toward her was Chick Uldridge, the stage manager. "Chick," she called and motioned him to her.

When he came up to her, Elaine spoke again. "Mr. Sellert was just leaving and, Chick, until further notice, this set is closed to anyone without a pass."

"Yes, ma'am," Chick said with an unreadable expression on his face. "Mr. Sellert?" Chick stepped back to let the film's ex-producer pass by, and Elaine watched them both until Sellert was out the door and Chick had spoken to the guard.

Breathing a sigh of relief, Elaine did her best to forget Sellert's words and concentrate on the rehearsal.

She watched Brandon walk through a short scene, and then watched Cindy do the same. Soon she was able to fully concentrate on the acting, and had indeed forgotten the incident with Sellert. About an hour later the director called a lunch break, and the cast and crew began to wander off in their separate directions.

Elaine went over to Hart, who was on the phone, and waited until the director was finished before speaking to him.

"They seemed to know their lines well enough," she ventured.

"For now," he replied.

"Is there a problem with the cast?"

"Not with the cast," Hart said, looking directly into her eyes.

"What's your problem now?" Elaine asked sharply.

"This is my set, and I will thank you to remember that.

The next time you decide to throw someone out, make sure I haven't invited them in the first place, Miss Producer.''

Holding down a fast surge of anger, Elaine forced a smile to her lips. ''And, Mr. Director, as the producer of this film, I have overall responsibility for everything that happens here. Mr. Sellert has been barred from the set. Is that clear?''

Anger suffused Hart's face, but a moment later all traces of it had fled. ''Perfectly,'' he said.

Brandon had spotted Elaine walking toward the director, and he'd started after her. He stopped just within hearing distance when Hart had snapped at Elaine. Brandon was no stranger to arguments between producers and directors, and he knew the wisdom of staying out of them, but he wasn't in an impersonal position anymore, and the director's anger bothered him. Deciding to interrupt, he started forward.

''Elaine, excuse me, but I need to speak to you for a minute.''

Elaine covered her surprise well, and nodded first at Brandon and then at Hart. She was happy to be able to get away from Hart, but her tension returned instantly when Brandon's hand touched her arm.

''What was that about?'' he asked when they were far enough away from the director.

''Personality conflict,'' she replied tersely.

''Are you okay?''

''I'm fine. Thanks for the rescue.''

''Lunch?'' Brandon asked.

''Sorry,'' she replied with a tight smile, ''but I have a meeting with the director of photography. He has a problem with one of the locations.''

"I'll accept that. How about dinner?" he asked as they neared the door.

"I'm sorry, Brandon. No."

"Soon, Elaine, soon," he stated firmly.

Elaine shook her head and willed her feet to move. A few moments later Brandon was gone. She knew her reactions to him were bad for her, and she knew she had to learn to control herself better. Then she realized that her anger at John Hart's presumptuous manner had disappeared as soon as Brandon had spoken to her. That, she decided, had been good.

Chapter 6

THE FIRST WEEK OF SHOOTING A MOVIE WAS ALWAYS THE most hectic for Elaine. Up until this film, she hadn't realized the full extent of what it meant to be the producer. As an assistant producer she had always had a set routine to follow and formulated jobs to do, but as the producer, every aspect of the filming was her responsibility.

After the first day of rehearsals, Elaine hadn't returned to the sound stage. Instead, she worked in her office, tying up loose ends and checking and rechecking every detail of the project to make sure that there would be no problems when the cameras rolled.

Then, as she had watched the first day of filming, she'd been called to a meeting by David Leaser. It was a publicity and advertising meeting that should have been held off for at least two months, but David Leaser had wanted to get an early start on *Distant Worlds*.

By the time the meeting ended tempers had grown raw.

The head of publicity had wanted to launch a strong campaign while the movie was in production. It was an old ploy that was used to whet appetites and make a movie a big seller before it was even released. Elaine had argued against it, saying it would put too much pressure on the cast and crew.

The publicity director and Elaine came close to blows, and only then had David Leaser stepped in. He had sided with Elaine to a degree and said that they would wait until at least half the filming was in the can before making a firm decision.

After the meeting Elaine cornered her boss and demanded an explanation for what had happened at the meeting. David had smiled and shaken his head slowly.

"Lanie, we're all pawns in a big game."

"Exactly what is that supposed to mean?" she asked, genuinely puzzled by his remark.

"You and I are on the creative end of the business, but the people who have invested in our company are the ones who make the demands. Our investors want to see more money than they have lately, and advance publicity is one way to boost profits."

"But this is ridiculous," she protested.

"Nothing is ridiculous when it involves eighteen million dollars."

He didn't have to add that the figure was only accurate if Elaine brought the movie in on schedule and on budget, but Elaine understood that. "I guess not," she replied, accepting what he'd said, realizing that Trion Studios, unlike her father's production company, was a public corporation whose employees were at the beck and call of the stockholders.

"I understand everything is going well," David said conversationally.

"It was when I left. They were setting up the first filming sequence."

"What do you think of Brandon Michaels?"

"I'll let you know the answer to that in five months," Elaine replied. She had exerted a major effort to keep her voice light and hoped it had worked.

"Elaine, I've already told you how important this movie is to me. And I know how you feel about not having control over the casting, among other things. Just do this movie, and do it well, and I promise you your own head on the next one."

Elaine looked at David steadily for a moment before she nodded her head in acceptance. "Even if you hadn't said that, I would have done my best. But thanks for the next film. I'll hold you to it," she stated in a deadly serious tone.

"You do that," he replied, just as seriously. Then he turned and went to his office. Before she returned to the set, she stopped in her office, and found Bonnie yelling frantically on the phone. By the time she calmed Bonnie down, she learned that there was yet another problem with the location arrangements in Death Valley.

The motel outside Barstow had made a mistake and wouldn't have enough rooms for the entire crew. Telling Bonnie that she would handle it, Elaine went into her office, her finely tuned senses warning her that this phone call was only the beginning. Her intuition proved correct, and Elaine found herself unable to leave her office until after nine that night.

But that had been a blessing in disguise, she realized the next day when she watched another scene being shot. For each time she was on the sound stage, she had been forced to watch Brandon, and to acknowledge that with every move he made, the truth of his words struck her over and over again.

She did love him.

Then, after three hectic days, Elaine found herself with some free time, which enabled her to go to the set and sit and watch the filming without being disturbed. The atmosphere in the sound stage that afternoon was permeated with excitement and action. Cameras were turning to follow the actors' movements, and the sound technicians' eyes never left their gauges. The only voices that could be heard were those of Brandon Michaels and Cynthia Reed as they spoke their lines to each other. The unused portions of the cavernous sound stage were dark in comparison to the brightly lit area used for this scene.

Elaine sat comfortably in her canvas chair, less than five feet from John Hart, who was watching the actors with unfeigned intensity. The scene was a fast-paced dialogue between Brandon and Cynthia, involving innuendos and double entendres and calling for a vast range of expressions and emotions. Watching carefully, Elaine was soon caught up in the witty exchange, and was surprised when John Hart's voice rang out.

"And . . . Cut!" cried the director. The background lights came on, and the two actors turned to face the director. "I think that'll be a take. Nice scene," he added.

Brandon smiled at Cynthia, and then started toward Hart. "Anything else today?" he asked.

The bearded director shook his head. "But be ready for the death scene in the morning. Don't shave," he reminded the actor.

"No problem," Brandon replied with a friendly grin.

He stepped past the director and paused when he spotted Elaine sitting in her chair.

Brandon had done his best to avoid her, especially after her rebuff at the first rehearsal, but seeing her every day had stretched his nerves close to the breaking point. He had to find a way to make her understand, to make her accept what he knew they both felt.

Elaine's breath caught when she saw Brandon coming toward her. Since that night at her house, she had avoided him whenever possible. When contact between them had been unavoidable, she'd spoken only about business, and had made sure that there were other people around. Glancing about, Elaine saw that, for the moment, the area was deserted and she would have to face him alone. Suddenly her throat was dry, as were her hands.

"Can we talk?" he asked when he reached her chair.

"Is there a problem?" Elaine asked quickly, too quickly.

"Yes."

"Oh? Is your dressing room big enough? Do you need a limousine?" she inquired sarcastically.

"What I need is some courtesy," Brandon rejoined caustically.

Elaine bit back her next words and slowly nodded her head. The tension gripping her was almost unbearable and she struggled to make herself relax.

"I don't like seeing you and not being able to talk freely," Brandon said.

"Perhaps we should try to be friends while we work together," Elaine suggested.

"Why are you so afraid of yourself?" he asked.

"It's not me that I fear."

"Your emotions, then."

Elaine looked around and saw that they were still alone. She couldn't believe that with almost a hundred people wandering around on the set nobody was closer than twenty feet away.

"My emotions are my business, Mr. Michaels. Now, if you'll excuse me, I have some paperwork to attend to." Elaine rose and started to walk away, but before she could take a step, Brandon's steel-like fingers were clamped around her wrist.

She turned to meet his eyes, challenge blazing from hers. They faced each other silently until, at last, he released her.

"I know you love me," he whispered.

Elaine stiffened, and then willed her muscles to relax, even as she curved her lips in a soft smile. "I had a pet spider once. It was a big, hairy tarantula. I loved him, but I kept him in a glass cage so he couldn't get out to bite me. Good day, Brandon." Elaine spun on her heels and walked toward the door of the sound stage, very conscious of Brandon's incredulous stare. But as she approached the door, she heard his deep, full laughter reaching out to taunt her.

Cynthia Reed stopped her car two feet away from Elaine's bumper. She shut off the engine but didn't leave the car immediately. She had to speak to Elaine, but how was her problem. Although Simon had trusted her with Elaine and Brandon's story, she couldn't just announce that she knew the circumstances. Elaine had always been a very private person, and Cindy didn't want her to think that she'd been spying on her.

But Cindy had been very much aware of the change in her friend during the last months, and had especially noticed Elaine's tense reactions whenever Brandon was nearby. Earlier that afternoon, she'd seen Elaine and Brandon talking on the set, and had seen also just how badly Brandon had affected her friend. It was then that she'd decided to speak to Elaine, to try to help her out. *If she'll let me.* Shrugging her shoulders, Cynthia left the car and went to the front door of Elaine's apartment.

She rang the bell, but when Elaine didn't answer, she opened her purse and took out the set of keys Elaine had given her. Their friendship was a long-standing one, and whenever Elaine was out of town, Cindy took care of her plants. Elaine did the same for Cindy.

Opening the door, Cindy went inside. Two minutes later she emerged on the rear deck, and looked toward the almost dark beach. She saw a silhouetted figure walking in the distance, and guessed it to be Elaine.

The night had almost descended, held back only by the slowly fading tentacles of pink and gray that Elaine didn't notice as she walked aimlessly along the beach, her hands tucked into the pouchlike pockets of her sweat shirt, her head lowered, watching the sand she kicked ahead of herself.

All her doubts about her abilities as a woman and as a producer swam in the unsettled mire that churned in her mind. Today had been the hardest day yet. She had faced Brandon, and had managed to ignore the yearning messages her heart had sent her, preferring instead to snap foolishly at him in an effort to pretend his words were untrue.

She remembered the way his taunting laugh had followed her from the sound stage. But she remembered as well, the fleeting pain that had crossed his face at her unkind words. She knew she had used them defensively, but that was no excuse. *I have to talk to him again, I have to explain myself,* she thought. Then she realized that she didn't understand herself enough to explain what was wrong with her.

She wanted him as she'd never thought it possible to want a man, and she feared him with the same degree of intensity. *How can I love someone I fear?* she wondered. Or—had what he'd said earlier been the truth—was she afraid of herself?

"I don't know!" Elaine yelled the words to the sea, but the sea didn't respond.

"They say that talking to yourself is a sign of greatness," Cindy said when she caught up to her friend.

Elaine jumped at the sound of Cindy's voice, and then turned to face her friend. "Just ask me to quit if you don't like me as your producer, don't try to scare me to death. And that's not all they say about people who talk to themselves," Elaine added, making a circular motion near her temple with her forefinger.

"You're as sane as I am," Cindy declared with a smile, "and you're a damn good producer."

"Thanks for the last part, anyway. What brings you over?"

"You," Cindy said honestly.

"I'm flattered . . . I think," Elaine joked.

"You should be. After all, I did come a long way to see you."

"Six and a half miles."

"Distance is more than distance," Cindy said philosophically, looking at Elaine. But neither of them could keep a straight face after that line, and they both laughed freely.

"And just where did you dig that one up?" Elaine asked.

"It was a line I had in a TV mini-series. It bombed—the line and the show," Cindy added.

"I can't imagine why," Elaine said dryly.

"Seriously, Lanie, it's been a while since we spent some time together. I just wanted to come and visit."

Elaine gazed knowingly at her friend, and then nodded her head. She knew Cindy well enough to see that there was something else, but she could wait it out. In the meantime, she was glad for the company. For some reason she didn't want to be alone tonight.

"Stay for dinner?" she asked.

"Love to."

"Cindy . . ."

"Yes?" Cindy asked, reading a mood shift in the tone of Elaine's voice.

"What are they saying about me?" she asked.

Cindy knew who Elaine meant by "they," but she stared out at the dark horizon for a moment before she spoke. "Does it matter?"

"If it didn't you wouldn't be here, and I wouldn't ask."

"We seem to have a divided cast and crew. But it's primarily the directorial end who seem to resent you."

"Hart."

"He's Sellert's friend, and you were pretty heavy-handed with Sellert," Cindy stated.

Elaine nodded, accepting the responsibility for her actions without making any excuses. "And?"

"It's a pretty well-known fact that you're Larry Rodman's daughter."

"So everyone thinks I'm riding on my father's coattails?"

"Not everyone, but they're all watching you carefully."

"Waiting to see me fall on my face!" Elaine said.

"I never realized you were a pessimist," Cindy snapped quickly.

"What else am I supposed to be?"

"What you always were, a smart person. Lanie, all you have to do is your job. You don't have to prove anything to anyone," Cindy advised.

"I wish it was that simple."

Cindy paused, and forced Elaine to face her eye to eye. She smiled at her friend, then reached out and took both of Elaine's hands in hers and squeezed them gently. "It is. Forget Hart's attitude, forget that Sellert was the one who started this film and just do your job. Dammit, Lanie, you're good, very good!"

Elaine smiled at Cindy, accepting the warmth of her words. "You're right, and I've been letting a lot of things get under my skin that shouldn't."

Elaine had spoken truthfully, and once the words were out, her tension began to abate. Most of it had to do with the movie, but Brandon's part in her life added to the anxiety.

"Lanie," Cindy said, releasing her friend's hands and turning to look out at the ocean, "what do you think of Simon Arnold?"

"I don't know. He's nice enough, intelligent, very different from most screenwriters. His ego doesn't get in the way of necessary changes, which is very nice."

"I mean as a person," Cindy persisted.

Elaine stared at the back of her friend's head for a moment before she realized what Cindy was getting at. "I think he's very nice, from what I know of him."

Cindy turned to Elaine with a smile on her face. "So do I."

"I didn't know," Elaine said softly.

"Well, we've been seeing each other for the last few weeks. I really like him."

" 'Like'?" Elaine asked.

"For now. We'll see what happens in the future."

Cindy paused for a moment, and Elaine saw her brow wrinkle with concentration. It was a telltale sign that Elaine had known for many years, signaling to her that Cindy had something on her mind that she was afraid to bring up.

"What?" Elaine prodded.

"It's not really any of my business . . ."

"Then you wouldn't be trying to figure out a way to say it. We've been friends for too long, Cynthia Reed. Just speak what's on your mind."

"All right," Cindy said. She took a deep breath, then spoke. "It's about Brandon and you."

"Bran—What about Brandon and myself?" Elaine asked in a louder voice than she had intended. As soon as Cindy had spoken his name, she knew her friend had discovered her secret.

"That's what I'm trying to find out," Cindy said, hoping that her white lie would never be discovered. "Lanie, I've seen the way you look at him when you think no one is watching you. And I've seen the way he looks at you. To me, it's obvious that something's going on between the two of you. I doubt that anyone else can tell, though, except for Simon."

"Simon?"

"Simon is as close to Brandon as I am to you."

Elaine couldn't stop the laugh that bubbled out, born of

the relief Cindy's words had produced. "You would only have noticed if Simon had mentioned that something had happened between Brandon and myself."

"You're wrong. I would have noticed, but having inside information helped. Do you want to talk about it?" Cindy asked in a low voice.

"Talk about what?" Elaine asked evasively as she stared out at the empty beach.

Cindy decided to plunge headfirst into the problem. "Lanie, you've been uptight for months, and this film is really important to you. There's something bothering you, and badly, too, and no amount of denials or evasions are going to hide it from me. We've known each other too long. Lanie, what's really bothering you?"

Elaine gazed at the one person who had always had the ability to see through whatever facade Elaine chose to wear, who could get her to admit the truth.

Suddenly the past four months of anger, hurt, uncertainty and self-doubt rushed to the surface. Blinking back the moisture that was filling her eyes, Elaine began to speak, opening the dam that held back her emotions, and let them out in a flooding rush as she told Cindy everything.

Wisely, Cindy said nothing about what she already knew; she just listened to her friend and silently accepted the love and trust that Elaine was bestowing upon her by sharing her troubles.

By the time Elaine had finished her story the sun had dropped behind the horizon, and dark streaks of purple decorated the sky. Hand in hand, Elaine and Cynthia returned to the house.

They ate a light dinner and afterward sat in the living room, discussing the movie. Neither brought up the subject of Brandon Michaels again. Cindy went home at eleven, and Elaine went to bed, hoping to sleep without dreaming of Brandon or feeling his touch or crying out his name, as she had found herself doing these past nights. *Just sleep*, she prayed as she shut the light.

Thursday had come and gone with another round of fast-paced and somewhat productive meetings, which had enabled Elaine to stay away from the set. And today, Friday, had been just as hectic. Luckily Jason Heller was a responsible, hard-working assistant producer whom Elaine could trust, having worked with him before.

And, Elaine thought honestly, the producer's *real* job was to stay out of the way of the cast and crew, but be there for support, and to make sure that there were no major problems. In that, she was doing her job well.

The intercom's loud signal broke Elaine's concentration, and she resignedly pressed the button. "Yes?"

"They're ready to screen the rushes," Bonnie said.

"On my way," Elaine replied. Rising, Elaine stretched to loosen the tension in her muscles and left the office. Although she had seen the dailies she wanted to see the first week's work all at one time. To that end, she'd asked that today's filming be developed quickly.

At the door of the screening room she found John Hart and his assistant director talking with Jason and another production assistant.

"Ready?" Jason asked when he saw her.

Elaine nodded, not missing the quick turn the director executed, crassly entering the screening room before her. Elaine shook her head and smiled at Jason's uplifted eyebrows, but didn't speak.

Once they were seated, Elaine nodded to Jason, who

told the projectionist to run the film. The screening room darkened and the screen lit up.

The first coding numbers ran across the screen, and then the close-up of the scene board popped into view. Elaine sat back and concentrated on the film, on the quality of the acting, sound and photography.

A half hour later the lights came on, only a hairbreadth after Elaine had regained her equilibrium. It was not the movie that had affected her so forcefully; rather, it was the power and strength Brandon had possessed on the screen that had reached out and struck her strongly. Brandon Michaels, on film, was a force to be reckoned with.

"Not bad," said the director.

"It was very good," Elaine stated. "The deathbed scene was magnificent, John."

"Ah, praise from upon high," Hart said with a smile that only emphasized the undertone in his voice. "Any other business tonight, or are we free for the weekend?"

Elaine held her temper back and forced a smile to her lips. "No more business," she said evenly.

"Good night, then," Hart said as he walked past Elaine, with the AD and the production assistant hot on his heels.

"You're free too, Jason," she said. "Thanks for all your help this week."

"You're welcome. See you Monday," he said cheerfully.

Elaine closed her eyes as he left, banishing John Hart's obvious crudeness, thinking only about the rushes she'd just seen.

"Will you need me anymore tonight, Miss Rodman?" came the faraway voice of the projectionist.

"Thank you, no, just leave the lights on."

"'Night," he called.

"'Night," Elaine replied absently as her thoughts returned to the film, and to Brandon.

Behind her, the screening room door opened and closed quickly, but she didn't hear it; she had become lost within the memory of the footage she had just seen.

From the first moment that Brandon's profile had filled the screen, her heart had twisted painfully, and she'd fought off the urge to raise her hand to his larger-than-life image to caress his cheek. His handsome face had seemed to reach out from the screen and come to her, his green eyes intent. Suddenly Elaine had become two people. With the analytical portion of her brain, she'd watched the film. But her emotional side had made her feel again the powerful physical sensations that had been awakened by him in New York.

When the dailies had ended, she'd still been a woman torn in two, and when she was at last alone in the screening room, she allowed herself to give in to the call of her heart. With her eyes closed and her heart crying with her loss, she strained to renew the conviction that she mustn't allow Brandon to penetrate the shield she had erected.

She recalled her conversation with Cindy the other night on the beach, and tried to forget her friend's words. But in this, too, she failed.

"Only you can say that what happened in New York was a mistake. Only you can convince yourself of that. Don't try to convince me," Cindy had warned with a shake of her head, "because I can't believe your words when I see the way you look at him."

Was she right? Am I fooling myself? Taking a deep, rasping breath, Elaine tried to comprehend the kaleidoscope of her emotions, unaware that she was not alone in the sound-proofed screening room.

Earlier that afternoon, Brandon had heard that there would be a closed screening of the week's rushes, and he knew that Lanie would be there. She had successfully avoided him for most of the week, and he had not pursued her after their one confrontation on Wednesday. But tonight he wanted to see her, and the screening of the week's filming was the perfect opportunity.

The last scene of the day had been filmed right after lunch, and by two o'clock Brandon was removing the last traces of his makeup. Instead of leaving, as did most of the cast and crew, Brandon had remained in his dressing room, going over the script changes for the following week. During lunch he had overheard the director complaining about Elaine's calling a closed screening of the rushes for five o'clock. It had been then that he'd decided to see them, and also to see her.

At five minutes after five, he'd gone not to the screening room, which he wouldn't have been allowed to enter, but to the projectionist's booth. He'd held a finger to his lips, silencing the projectionist.

"I want to see how I did," he'd whispered conspiratorially.

The projectionist hadn't argued, and Brandon had guessed he was not the first to do this sort of thing.

He'd watched the rushes, and had been pleased with his performance. Then he'd heard the way John Hart had spoken to Elaine, forcing himself not to get angry at the presumptious manner of the director.

He'd waited until everyone was gone, and when he realized Elaine wasn't leaving, he left the booth with the projectionist, but instead of leaving the building he'd gone to the door of the screening room, opening it gently.

Elaine hadn't heard him. Walking quietly, he approached the woman who was so deeply lost in thought.

"Lanie," he whispered.

Elaine heard her name spoken from a thousand miles away. Slowly, she chased away her thoughts, and turned toward the voice. As soon as she saw Brandon standing near her, she froze, aware of her heart's sudden quickening.

"Did you like the scenes?" he asked with a serious expression on his face.

"What are you doing here?" she asked, ignoring his question, trying to recover her composure.

"Taking an opportunity when it presents itself," he told her truthfully.

Elaine took a deep breath and came to her feet to face him. But he was too close to her; she could feel his powerful aura surrounding her like an all-encompassing blanket. "Why can't you accept what I've said?" Elaine asked, trying to stay unemotional.

"It's not in my nature to accept defeat," he informed her with yet another crooked grin. His eyes swept across her features, drinking in their beauty as he spoke.

Elaine refused to fall under his spell, refused to give in to the tugging of her heart. "No, of course not," she snapped sarcastically. "Your nature is to win at all costs, isn't it?"

Brandon continued to smile as he slowly raised his hand. When his fingertips grazed her cheek, Elaine snapped her head back as if she'd been burned. "Don't," she pleaded.

"Still afraid?"

"You conquered me once, wasn't that enough to satisfy your ego? Or do I have to fall at your feet in obsequious servility?" she demanded, losing the control she had fought so valiantly to retain.

"You're wrong, again."

Elaine gazed at him, and then at the closed door.

"No one will disturb us here. The door's locked and the room's sound-proofed. No one will find out your terrible secret."

"Brandon, what do you want from me?" she asked hesitantly.

"You," he said simply, his hand reaching toward her again.

Elaine's head spun dangerously, and she couldn't stop the twisting in her stomach. "Why?" she whispered.

"Elaine, I've told you that already," he said. He stroked her satin-skinned cheek with the backs of his fingers.

Wherever his fingers brushed her face, her nerve endings sparked. The love and desire that she had been denying was coming closer to the surface, and she began to tremble in reaction.

Then his hand left her face, and just as suddenly she felt herself captured within his arms, her breasts crushed to his hard chest.

"Brandon!" she cried, but her words were cut off when his lips touched hers. Lightning and thunder broke loose within her head and the passions she had been withholding broke lose to engulf her and destroy the last shreds of her self-control.

The intensity of his kiss robbed her of breath. The pounding of her pulse, the blood pulsing through her veins, were the only sounds she heard. The kiss lasted forever, and even as her mind struggled against it, her body turned traitor, responding eagerly to Brandon's embrace.

Finally, when his lips lifted from hers and the world became steady again, Elaine looked into his eyes.

"You can't lie to me, or to yourself, any longer," Brandon whispered huskily. "You can't."

Elaine took a deep breath, then carefully backed away from him, his hands falling away from her body. When she realized she was truly free of his hold, she stopped, aware of the way her breasts rose and fell, of the fierce beating of her heart.

Suddenly she knew she had to speak the truth. "No, I can't," Elaine admitted. "I've loved you from the moment we met. But I know what my life must be, and you can't be a part of that."

Brandon stared at her, his eyes accusatory in their intensity. "Semantics, Lanie. You're playing with words."

"Which you know a great deal about, don't you?" she challenged.

"I also know about love," he said.

"Seduction would be a better word!"

Brandon's control snapped, and his anger flared dangerously. "I had forgotten how one-sided that night was. I had forgotten how I took you so unwillingly," he said, his indolently handsome mouth curving in a sneer.

Elaine reacted as if she'd been slapped. Her face turned scarlet with humiliation, and her eyes misted until Brandon and the screening room blurred before her.

"Damn you," she whispered.

Brandon stared at her, almost but not quite sorry for his words. "It takes two people to have a love affair, Elaine, two people who care about each other enough to overcome their problems.'' Then he came to her, his arms going around her, not in a greedy, passionate way, but gently, securely. ''All I'm asking is that we try.''

Elaine stood stiffly within his grasp. Although she could feel the heat of his body through her clothing, and was almost overwhelmed by his nearness, she sensed she had nothing to fear.

''Brandon, I don't know,'' she told him truthfully.

''Dinner. Just have a quiet dinner with me tonight. Let's talk like people, not like gladiators trying to kill one another.''

His words struck a chord deep within her, and for the first time since she had become aware of his presence, she relaxed. ''Just dinner and talk?'' she asked in a low voice.

''Yes.''

''All right,'' she said, aware of the swift lightening of her heart. And aware, too, of the sudden surge of anticipation that followed.

Chapter 7

MONDAY MORNING, AND THE THIRD WEEK OF FILMING, had come with the suddenness of a vacation's end. The weekend had flown by faster than Elaine had thought possible, and had brought with it a new feeling of acceptance of their relationship. They had seen each other three nights in a row, and she had reveled in his presence. But as she found herself falling more and more in love with him, she had held herself back, made herself wait to see if this was real or just a fantasy.

She sat in a chair near the set, the day's script unopened on her lap. Elaine saw nothing of the flurry of movement around her; instead, her mind had retreated in thought, once again focusing on the weekend that had just passed.

Of all the problems she could foresee between them, the one that continued to haunt her was her inability to be two people at once. She loved Brandon and she loved her work. Elaine wondered how she would be able to walk the thin line between being in love with Brandon and being the producer of his film.

For the past three nights, Brandon had been so wonderful, so caring, that her love for him seemed to grow whenever she even thought of him. Each night had shown her a new facet of the handsome man, and she'd sensed a multitude of discoveries she had yet to make.

But her biggest surprise had been at the end of each evening, when Brandon had kissed her good night and left her at her front door. Not once had she been forced to offer any resistance to his advances, for there had been none. It was as though he'd understood that what had happened in New York was to be forgotten. And yet it was not as if they were starting over; it was merely that they were waiting until the time was right for them to show each other their love.

When will that be? she wondered. Elaine knew now, without any reservation, that she loved Brandon deeply. But her hesitation was brought on by her past experiences. She didn't want to be used, not by anyone! At the same time, Elaine realized that she had never wanted a man the way she did Brandon. She wanted to make love with him, but she was afraid. Taking a deep breath, trying to clear her mind, Elaine concentrated on the bustle around her.

The sound stage was a beehive of activity, with grips moving to and fro, makeup artists and hairdressers applying the finishing touches to the actors, who were about to shoot a scene, and stagehands double-checking the props and scenery.

Sitting in the chair imprinted with her name, Elaine returned her attention to the shooting script of the scene about to be filmed, watching the preparations from the corners of her eyes.

John Hart paced nervously in front of Cynthia, explaining again the way he felt the scene should be played, striking one fist into an open palm to emphasize his words.

A loud crash from behind her made Elaine jerk her head around. One of the extras had tripped over a sound wire, and fallen against a prop. She shook her head, then looked back at the script.

A moment later the assistant director called for quiet. Putting aside the script, Elaine sat up and studied the set. It was a mock-up of the library in the house they'd chosen for exterior shots, a large Victorian mansion.

Brandon was already in position, standing by the fireplace, about to light the logs. His face was set in lines of deep concentration, and Elaine knew he had put himself fully into the part.

"Quiet on the set," Hart called. Instant silence descended at his command. "All right, roll it," he told the AD.

"Scene twelve, take one, *Distant Worlds,* and . . . action!" the assistant director shouted. A second later the clipboard's quick snap signaled the start of filming.

Lights blazed on, and Elaine watched Brandon strike a match and drop it into the fire. He turned on cue, just as Cynthia stepped into the library, and took a step toward her.

Then all hell broke loose. A loud explosion filled the air, and at the same instant, a blinding flash of light shot out from the fireplace. Elaine, frozen in her seat, could only watch.

Flames spewed from the fireplace, showering Brandon

with sparks. Feeling the first shock wave of the explosion and seeing Cynthia's eyes widen in fear, Brandon launched himself into the air. He landed on top of Cynthia, pulling her face into his chest and covering her body with his own, protecting her as best he could.

Elaine's mind screamed in horror as she galvanized her body into action. Leaping from her chair, her heart pounding with fear for Brandon and Cynthia, she ran on to the set. The startled screams and shouts of the crew were muted in her ears—her only thought was for their safety.

Chick Uldridge, the stage manager, ran toward them with a fire extinguisher. But Elaine reached the set first and, grabbing a small area rug lying near the fallen actors, she flung it over the two huddled forms, effectively putting out the flames that were feeding on the back of Brandon's jacket.

A half dozen hands reached past her to lift off the carpet, and another stagehand released a jet of carbon dioxide, making sure that Brandon and Cynthia were safe.

Elaine's blood raced madly, adrenaline surging through her. Her breathing was labored as she stared frantically at the forms of the two people dearest to her. *Please let them be all right,* she prayed. Then Simon Arnold burst through the crowd and dropped to his knees beside them, reaching out to help them up.

Brandon shook his head as he lifted himself off Cynthia's body. He felt hands under his arms, lifting him, and saw Simon's concerned face near his as his friend reached down to Cindy. Then he glanced up into Elaine's tense face and fearful eyes.

"Brandon," she whispered, her voice cracking.

Brandon moistened his lips with his tongue, then smiled

tentatively. "Can I light a fire, or can I light a fire?" he joked as his smile became one of reassurance. With his eyes still on her, he shrugged out of his charred jacket.

Relieved that he was all right, yet knowing she couldn't throw herself into his arms, she nodded slowly and turned to Simon. Cynthia, who was huddled in his arms, was shaking uncontrollably.

"Cindy?" she ventured. When she stepped closer to her friend, she saw that Cynthia was more frightened than hurt.

"I'm . . . I'm okay," she whispered. "Brandon, thank you," she said, looking at her co-star.

Brandon nodded, but said nothing. The set was quiet again.

"Dammit all!" screamed John Hart as he surveyed the damage. "We'll have to rebuild the set."

"That's better than starting from scratch, with different actors," Elaine snapped, giving vent to her nervousness.

Hart whirled to face her, his features twisted in an angry scowl. But when his eyes met hers, he shook his head and relaxed. "Sorry. You're right. We're lucky that no one was hurt."

Elaine nodded, accepting his apology. When she turned to look for Brandon, she saw him hunched over the remains of the fireplace with Chick Uldridge.

"Chick," Elaine called as she started toward him. The stage manager straightened and met her halfway. "What happened?"

"I don't know, Miss Rodman. I was just trying to find out."

"Maybe you should call security."

"No need," said Brandon as he held up a fragmented

piece of metal that he'd wrapped in a piece of cloth to protect himself from being burned. "It seems that someone got careless. They left a can of kerosene too close to the logs. When I threw the match in, the first flames probably ignited the fumes from the can."

Chick Uldridge stared intently at the metal Brandon held, his features a tight mask. "I'll check on it," he muttered.

Elaine turned from the wreckage to look around the sound stage. "Can you have everything cleaned up by the morning?" she asked Chick.

"You can count on it," he replied firmly.

"Good. Can I have everyone's attention?" Elaine called. All movement on the set stopped and all eyes went to the producer. "I want all crew members to check their equipment. If there are any damages, let me know immediately. Everyone else is free to go home. We'll resume shooting tomorrow morning."

The cast and crew began to move lethargically toward either their equipment or the dressing rooms, everyone obviously still in states of shock at the frightening accident.

Elaine turned to her assistant and rapidly fired off further instructions. "Jason, I want to see the production staff and the directorial staff in the meeting room in an hour."

Jason Heller nodded and quickly went to inform each of the people involved. Only then did Elaine return to Brandon. "Are you sure you're all right?"

"I'm fine," he assured her.

"Perhaps you should see the studio doctor. . . ."

"I'm fine. But I am concerned about you."

"Thank you," she whispered.

"No. Thank *you*. That carpet saved me from being burned. A few seconds later and . . ."

"You saw," she whispered, momentarily taken aback. She hadn't thought he'd seen her.

"I saw. Lanie . . ."

"I know," Elaine said quickly, nervously.

Brandon caught her concern and nodded. "We'll talk later."

"Yes, we will."

Then Simon, with Cynthia leaning on his arm, joined them. "Simon, will you take Cynthia over to the doctor?"

"I'm all right. Brandon made sure of that," Cindy said. "Thank you again."

Brandon nodded as Simon led her toward the dressing rooms. "Shall I walk you to your office?"

Elaine shook her head slowly. "I'll have to stop by David's office first and let him know what happened. Then I have the insurance papers to fill out, and then the meeting. I'll see you later."

"I'll pick you up?"

"Fine."

"Elaine . . ."

She gazed into his eyes and almost forgot where she was. "I . . . we'll talk later." Forcing herself not to give in to the desire to hold and kiss him, Elaine walked slowly toward the exit.

When she had gone, Brandon started toward his dressing room, but the stage manager stopped him.

"Mr. Michaels, I want you to know—"

"It's all right, Chick. No one was hurt." He knew Chick was taking the full responsibility for the accident. As stage manager, Chick was in charge of the sound stage.

"No, I wanted to tell you that I was the one who put the kerosene on the logs, and I didn't leave the can there."

"You're sure?" Brandon asked in a tight voice.

"I'm sure," Chick stated firmly.

Brandon searched the stage manager's face and decided he was telling the truth. "Don't say anything to anyone," Brandon ordered.

"But . . ."

"Do this for me, okay?"

"All right, Mr. Michaels, but it makes me nervous."

Brandon took a deep breath, then smiled shallowly. "Me too, Chick, me too."

Elaine studied the people sitting around the large table in Trion's main conference room. They had been there for half an hour, listening to the various reports concerning the set that had been destroyed. All in all, it wasn't too bad, Elaine realized as she glanced at the figures on her note pad. About $5000 worth of damage had been done to the set, but the damage had not extended to any other sets or props.

"Equipment?" she asked her assistant producer.

"One camera is being checked out. The sound recording system was overloaded. I've already gotten a replacement, but that's all the physical damage."

"All right. Chick?"

"The set will have to be rebuilt, of course."

"How long?"

"Two weeks."

"John, can we shoot today's scene after we've finished the location filming?" she asked the director. She knew he liked filming in sequence and was proud of his past record, which proved his ability to do just that.

"I don't think we have any choice," he said sardonically, shrugging his shoulders and giving the stage manager a sidelong glance. Apparently he had learned the cause of the explosion.

Elaine saw Chick's face flush and his neck muscles knot with tension. "I don't think accusations are called for. Accidents happen all the time," she stated.

"Not on my films!" Hart snapped.

"I think today proved differently," Elaine replied in a cool voice. "Now I want to bring something else up. Who called the papers?" She searched the faces intently.

"For a half hour before I came to this meeting I was fielding calls from every columnist in town. It seems that we have an open set, or perhaps a direct line to the gossip columnists!"

Elaine watched them all shift uncomfortably in their seats as they waited for her to continue. "I hope, in the future, we can keep our problems to ourselves—keep it in the family. Because if I find out who is leaking information, he or she will be out before they can count to three. Pass the word along," she ordered.

"Elaine," John Hart said in an even tone.

"John?"

"We have four more days of studio work, and then we're going to Death Valley. I'd like to take my staff there early to set up some of the angles."

"And?" she asked, unsure of what he was getting at. As the director he could do whatever he pleased at his end of the preparations.

"I'll need two cameramen and their equipment. You'll have to authorize the overtime."

"I see no prob—"

"Excuse me," Al Morton, the director of cinematography, cut in, "but that will put me over budget."

Although his words said one thing, his face said another, reminding Elaine of studio protocol. "I'll clear it," Elaine said, removing the responsibility from Al's shoulders. "But in the future, I'd appreciate it if you'd bring it up with Al first," she told Hart.

"Sorry," Hart said to Al Morton.

"Anything else?" she asked. When no one replied, Elaine rose. "Then I guess I'll see everyone bright and early tomorrow morning," she said as she walked from the room. Behind her, she heard John Hart's voice.

"Whatever you say, Miss Producer. . . ." came his taunting whisper.

Why is he fighting me so hard? she asked herself.

While Elaine held her meeting, Brandon stayed on the sound stage, once again looking over the damages. Then he returned to his dressing room, took off his makeup, changed into a pair of jeans and then found himself back on the set, looking at the destroyed fireplace and walls once more. His memory was sharp as to what had occurred, and he also remembered that Elaine, Chick and Simon had been the only ones to keep their wits and come instantly forward to help, while everyone else had been paralyzed.

He could still see Elaine's taut face, and felt another rush of emotion at the way her features eased when she had realized he was all right.

Brandon heard his name called, and turned to see Simon walking toward him through the debris.

"How's Cindy doing?"

"She's okay, just shaken up. She's still in her dressing room. I'm going to take her home as soon as she's changed."

"What do you think?" Brandon asked, looking around at the mess.

"I don't know," Simon replied. Then he shook his head slowly. "But I've got a strange question for you."

"Yes?"

"I don't want you to think I'm going crazy . . ."

"Simon, you can't *go* crazy if you already *are*," Brandon jested.

"Seriously. I don't know why, but I think there's something screwy going on."

"On the set?"

"Uh-huh."

"Because of what happened today?" Brandon asked, looking steadily at Simon.

"No, it doesn't really have anything to do with the accident. Remember how bitchy Hart was the first days of rehearsal?"

Brandon thought about it for a moment, and nodded.

"Don't you think it's strange how he's suddenly become Mr. Nice Guy?" He raised both his eyebrows to accent the question.

"It was probably just a case of nerves. You know how directors get when they start a new project."

"I know, and that's what I thought up until today. Did you see the way he reacted to the fire? He didn't give a damn that someone might have been hurt. His only concern was that he lost a day of shooting. Bran, I just have this feeling that something's not right with him."

"Don't let it throw you. This is Hollywood, not

Broadway. They do things differently here," Brandon suggested.

Before Simon could respond, Cindy walked onto the sound stage. "I'm ready," she told Simon. Then, glancing around, she shuddered visibly.

"Brandon," she said when her eyes reached him. "I want to thank—"

"You already did. Go home and forget about this," he told her.

But when Simon and Cynthia had gone, Brandon still couldn't leave. He thought about Simon's words and pondered the sudden change in John Hart's attitude. He would talk to Elaine about it tonight, he decided.

A cool breeze from the Pacific swept across the redwood deck of Brandon's house and caressed Elaine with its gentle salt spray. The silver cast of the crescent moon was set within a jeweled blanket of stars.

For Elaine, leaning against the railing, the peacefulness of the night was very different from her emotions. A strong tension, unlike anything she had ever experienced before, had charged the air between Brandon and herself with an electrical force from the moment he had arrived at her house tonight.

Elaine had tried to forget the events at the studio as best as she could. She knew, long before Brandon had arrived, that tonight would be a special night. Too much had happened today, she'd come too close to losing Brandon forever. When her doorbell had finally signaled his arrival, Elaine had been ready.

When she'd opened the door she had read the approval in his eyes as he'd gazed at her lightly made-up face, and then at the emerald silk dress she had chosen for their date. She'd been conscious of his eyes wandering along her body's contours, and had been thankful when they'd returned to meet hers, glowing softly.

The dress she wore had been made especially for her, a birthday present she had given to herself. It was very fashionable, and although it outlined her body perfectly, it still preserved a classic dignity. Although she couldn't wear a bra with it, the bodice had been designed to hide that fact. But the intensity of his stare had made her wonder if she should have chosen something a little less daring.

Forcing her thoughts elsewhere, Elaine remembered her arrival here tonight and her surprise at the beautiful house Brandon was living in.

"It's lovely, Brandon. How did you manage to rent it?" she'd asked when Brandon had pulled the car into the driveway.

"It's a long story. One that I *will* tell you one day," he promised.

Elaine did not pursue the topic; instead, she looked at the house, which was lit by floodlights that bathed its redwood exterior boldly yet unpretentiously. There was a large picture window near the front door, and as they pulled to a stop, Elaine had seen the slanting roof that told her she would find a cathedral ceiling in the living room.

The cry of a night bird broke into her concentration, taking her thoughts away from the house.

Brandon stepped onto the deck and approached Elaine. Before he reached her, he put two brandy snifters on the glass patio table, and paused to gaze at the outline of her figure. Her height against the dark sky, the soft curves of her waist and hips called to him in ways he'd never imagined.

Her short, gold-streaked hair was tossed by the same breezes that tugged at the silk of her dress, moving it in alluring patterns. His throat constricted when he thought of how close he'd come to losing her, but he shook away the thought and moved toward her.

When he was directly behind her he slipped his arms around her waist and clasped them together, inhaling the sweet fragrance of her perfume.

Elaine had sensed Brandon's presence behind her, and she did not jump when his arms wound around her. She covered his hands with hers and leaned her head back so that her cheek rested against his.

They stayed that way for several quiet moments, enjoying the stillness of the night and the pleasure of being together. "Are you happy?" Brandon asked, his deep voice soothing in her ear.

"I think so," Elaine replied honestly.

Loosening his arms, Brandon turned her to face him. "What will it take to make you certain?"

Elaine gazed into his eyes, her lips dry. With the darting tip of her tongue, she moistened them before she spoke.

"Time."

"Lanie, I want you," Brandon whispered huskily.

Elaine's breath caught in her throat and her body tensed. The heat of Brandon's body penetrated through their clothing, and the electricity springing from their closeness vibrated along her entire length.

"Brandon, I . . ."

"Why are you fighting me, and yourself? Are you that afraid of a commitment?"

Elaine stared at him as if she'd been struck. Of all the things he could have said, he had chosen the harshest. "Shouldn't I be?"

"Only if you don't trust yourself," Brandon whispered without moving his eyes from hers.

"I—" she began, but Brandon wouldn't let her continue; instead, he kissed her deeply.

The searing heat of his lips attacked her with a ferocity that left Elaine weak-kneed, holding on to Brandon to keep herself from falling. Then the darting entrance of his tongue into her mouth made her head swim madly and her arms tightened around him. The muscular leanness of his body, and the fires it ignited, could no longer be denied as Elaine began to return his kiss in a passionate response.

When the kiss ended, Elaine's sharp intake of breath was echoed by Brandon's. They stared at each other for a moment before his hand left her back to rise slowly upward, stopping when it cupped the back of her head.

"I want you," he repeated. Then his mouth was crushing hers, his fiery lips demanding, and his hands held her a suddenly willing prisoner.

All of Elaine's resistance fled under the intensity of his onslaught. Although Elaine knew how dangerous the waters could be, she dove into them recklessly, abandoning her reserve and offering Brandon her love without saying a word.

Brandon felt the tension flow from her body, and accepted the warmth she bestowed upon him as she returned his kiss passionately. As he cupped her head with one hand, his other one caressed her back in slow circles. Brandon could hardly breathe.

Stepping back, he reached out and took Elaine's hands in his. He smiled softly, trying to erase the concern he saw on her face, and to give her, at the same time, the confidence he so badly wanted both of them to have in each other.

In time, he told himself, wishing that Elaine could read his thoughts. Then he began to walk toward the doorway to the house, still holding her hand tightly.

Elaine followed him, her hand imprisoned within his larger one. With her heart beating so loudly she thought he must hear it, they walked through the elegant living room and up the stairs to what she knew must be the master bedroom.

Then they were inside. There was only a single light casting a soft glow through the room. Brandon drew her to him and again lowered his mouth to hers.

Elaine tasted the warm sweetness of his mouth, and felt again the lean power of his body against hers. The strength of his arms around her eased her fears. The growing seeds of her passion began to flower as their mouths remained locked together. Elaine cried out suddenly when Brandon pulled his lips from hers, but the deep smoldering look in his eyes quieted her distress.

Again he reached for her hand, and again Elaine placed hers within his. Not a word had been spoken since the first instant their lips had met on the deck outside. Now, within the confines of the large bedroom, Elaine knew she was where she wanted to be.

She walked toward the large bed as if in a dream, and when she was at its side she turned to gaze at Brandon. His face was shadowed, but the expression he wore gave Elaine the confidence to go on. Her hand trembled slightly when she raised it to his face, but he didn't notice as he took it and pressed it to his lips.

Brandon tasted the silken skin of her palm, then

released her hand and turned Elaine away from him. His fingers sought the dress's zipper, and he carefully undid it before turning her around to face him again.

Then he couldn't hold himself back, and he took her face in his hands. He kissed her deeply, letting the months of suppressed desire explode within the single kiss. Moments later, he reluctantly let her go, but continued to caress her face with his eyes.

Elaine was held captive by the green depths of his eyes, afraid to move and break the spell that enveloped them both. Her breathing had grown harsh and her mouth was dry. His hands, still cupping her face, were like blazing coals. Then they left her face to trail slowly along her neck before slipping under the material at her shoulders.

An instant later the silk dress lay crumpled at her feet, and all that stood between her and Brandon was the lace of her slip.

What she saw in his eyes ignited yet another fire within her, a fire that soon raged out of control. Elaine molded herself to Brandon, pressing against him with a need she had never known herself to possess. In that instant, with the material of his clothing rubbing against her bare breasts, she couldn't deny her emotions. She needed him now more than she had ever needed another person, and Elaine realized, too, that her yearning was not just that of sexuality—it was a much deeper desire.

Then he lifted her off her feet, and a heartbeat later she was lying on the bed. Brandon didn't move from her; he continued to kiss her deeply. His hands trailed along her body, and when his fingers caught the edge of her slip, his lips left hers. His mouth wandered downward along her neck, stopping often to kiss her soft skin. As his mouth moved between her breasts, scorching the valley, Elaine bit her lip to keep from crying out. Then Brandon, in sensuous movements, removed her slip and panties and stood at the edge of the bed.

Brandon's eyes roamed over Elaine, drinking in the lushness of her face and body as he removed his shirt. Then they returned to her face, and stayed locked with her eyes as he removed the rest of his clothing. Still without speaking, he went to the light on the far dresser.

Elaine heard the click of the switch, but instead of the darkness she expected, the room went from the yellow glow to a silver sheen. Looking up, she saw a skylight above the bed and the silver of the crescent moon.

He joined her on the bed, kissing her mouth, her eyes, her chin, before trailing his lips along her neck, feeling the pounding of her blood as it flowed beneath her skin. His hands and mouth worked in unison as he reacquainted himself with the perfection of her body. He devoured her, leaving nothing untouched, unkissed. Elaine trembled beneath his searching hands and mouth. Elaine felt him touch every inch of her. She luxuriated in the gentle yet forceful hands she had wanted for so long, the lips she needed, and the love she could no longer deny. Then he shifted, rising above her, his hair highlighted by silver flecks of reflected moonlight. The palms of her hands were suddenly on his hard, muscular chest as he began to lower himself on her.

But she felt him holding back. His eyes once again locked on hers, and she knew what he was waiting for. "Please," she whispered, moistening her dry lips with her tongue, "I love you."

She felt his hardness pierce her, driving deep and

pressing her down into the mattress. Elaine shuddered at the suddenness of their joining, even as she wrapped her arms and legs around him, securing him to her.

Brandon gazed into the face of the woman he wanted so much, and after long months of waiting, finally felt at peace with himself. His eyes drank in her every features as he made love to her, until he became lost inside her and lowered his lips to hers. The welcoming softness of her mouth added to his surging desire and the love that raged within his heart and mind.

Elaine gave up the thin control she'd fought to retain as she saw the sweeping emotions race across his face. She welcomed his hard, muscular body with hers, with the heat of her thighs, and the rippling of her stomach muscles against his. Deep within her, Elaine felt the powerful and fiery passions build, exploding wildly, sending lances of red-hot fire throughout her entire being.

Her fingers curled on his back as she grasped on to him tighter and tighter. Her mouth opened against his, and a low, throaty moan floated into the air. Her breasts were crushed, her nipples strained upward, teased and caressed by the dense mat of hair covering his chest. Then her body tensed under a surging wave of love and passion that began to carry her away.

Brandon was lost within the heated depths of Elaine's body, inhaling the subtle scent that was so much a part of her, feeling their love becoming a real and powerful force. Then he felt her tense around him, and his own passion erupted with a fury that shook him to his very core.

Wave after wave of indescribable pleasure engulfed Elaine, and she found she couldn't control her breathing. Brandon's weight rested upon her and she felt his heart beating in unison with hers. With their mingled breaths the only sounds in the room, she began to relax her body. Lifting her head slightly, she kissed him, and smiled at the tickling sensation of his hair on her lips. Then, with her head resting on the pillow and her eyes searching the heavens through the skylight, she stroked his soft, curly hair, glad that he was alive and lying next to her.

And she thought again of what had happened to Brandon today. She had been terrified when the fire had exploded outward, almost devouring him with its blast. She had reacted by instinct when she'd run to where he and Cynthia lay on the floor and covered them with the rug. Only later, in the privacy of her office, had the shock of the events gotten to her.

She had been sitting at her desk, staring out the window, when the realization hit her that Brandon could have died if he hadn't already turned his back to the fireplace.

She shivered, and felt Brandon's reassuring grip on her shoulders. "Cold?" he asked quickly.

"No," she whispered. Then she kissed him, not deeply, not passionately, but lovingly.

Chapter 8

THE INTERCOM'S BUZZ STARTLED ELAINE FROM THE PAGE of the script she was rereading. Absently, she pressed down the switch. "Yes?"

"Mr. Rodman on line four," Bonnie informed her.

"Thank you," she said, clicking off the intercom with one hand and picking up the phone with the other. "Hi, Dad."

"'Afternoon, Lanie. I just thought I'd check in and see how you were doing—especially since I haven't heard from you in over two weeks."

Elaine flushed at his gentle reproof, but smiled at the same time. "I've been so busy, I haven't kept track of the time. Sorry, Daddy," she said.

"I guess I can accept that. How's it going?"

"So far so good. Except for one scene, we're on schedule, and everyone is working hard."

"That one scene wouldn't be what I read about in the paper today, would it?"

"It wasn't as bad as they made it out to be," Elaine explained. Now she knew the real reason for her father's call. And she realized she should not only have expected to hear from him, but should have called him yesterday.

"I know, I spoke to David. An accident, it seems."

"One of the stagehands was careless. It won't happen again, I can promise you that."

"How's your star? Is he as hard to work with as the rumors say?"

"Brandon?" she asked in guilty surprise, caught off guard by the sudden switch in their conversation.

"I know Cynthia is easy to work with."

"Brandon is no problem. He's a professional through and through," she told him truthfully.

"I'm glad to hear that. By the way, I'm going to spend a few weeks at the ranch. Would you care to join me this weekend?"

Elaine looked at her calendar quickly before she answered. "Gee, Dad, I don't know. We're wrapping up the first of the basic studio work. Then next Tuesday we start filming on location."

"Then you have a three-day break this weekend," he said.

"That all depends on how smoothly the setup goes." As she spoke, she found herself thinking about her father's offer seriously, and she realized that she would indeed have some free time. "Let me see what I can arrange, okay?"

"That would be fine," her father replied.

"Can I invite some guests?"

"We have the room. Anyone special?"

"Why don't you wait and find out? I'll call you later and let you know."

"All right. Keep up the good work," Lawrence Rodman said as he hung up the phone.

"I'm trying, Daddy," Elaine whispered to the dial tone.

Elaine glanced again at the shooting calendar on her wall. There would be three days off, Saturday through Monday, and then shooting would resume on Tuesday at their first location, near Death Valley.

The past weeks had been hectic, filled with hours and hours of work; in that, she hadn't lied to her father. Then she thought of Brandon and what had happened between them last night.

The explosion of passion and love had been a revealing experience for Elaine. By the time she had fallen asleep in Brandon's arms, she had known her heart was no longer hers to control, but completely his. Then, sometime during the night, with the stars filling the glass of the skylight, they had made love again, a gentle love that had been a never-ending exploration filled with discoveries that surprised and pleased them both.

When she had woken this morning in Brandon's bed, she'd been perfectly happy, for there had been no red rose, no note in his place; there had been Brandon, turning to take her into his arms and kiss her deeply. With the dawn's first faint light, they had joined together in a slow, joyful surrender of love.

Perhaps it was time to introduce Brandon to her father, she thought. Elaine knew that the ranch would be the perfect place to do it. *The ranch,* she said to herself. What her father fondly called "the ranch" was exactly that, a

30,000-acre working ranch, with a large herd of prime cattle and a smaller herd of quarter-horse stock. Her father had bought the ranch twelve years ago as a second home, but had soon discovered that although he liked the life it offered, his commitments in business and his love of moviemaking prevented him from moving there.

Lawrence Rodman spent as much time at the ranch as possible, and Elaine did, too. It would be a nice place for Brandon and her father to meet, Elaine thought happily.

Shaking her head and forcing herself to concentrate on the script changes, Elaine began to read in earnest. The changes had been suggested by Brandon and Cynthia, and had to do with one particular scene. Elaine had agreed with them, and so had the director. They had gone to Simon who, unlike many writers, listened to what they had to say and made the appropriate changes swiftly.

The pages she was looking at now would be shot tomorrow. Sighing, Elaine checked off the last page and stood up. After she'd stretched, she went into the outer office and gave the script changes to Bonnie, who would have them copied and sent to the actors.

With that done, Elaine looked at her watch and saw that she had five minutes to get ready for the weekly production meeting with David Leaser. Afterward, she would go to the screening room to see the previous day's rushes. Only then would her long day be over. Elaine smiled as she found herself looking forward to spending a quiet evening with Brandon.

"That sounds like a wonderful idea," Brandon said, putting his coffee cup down and gazing across the table at Elaine.

"I'm glad you think so. I'll call my father in the

morning and tell him we'll be coming. Oh, would you mind if I invited Cindy?"

"And Simon?" he asked.

"Of course," she replied with a grin. "After all, they're an item."

Both Brandon and Elaine laughed nervously at her remark, not because it was true, but because it hit too close to home. For the past two days, the Hollywood gossip columns had been alive with references to the famous New York playwright and one of Hollywood's rising young stars. Today, one columnist had actually named Simon and Cynthia, making a big to-do over it, adding to the small article the fact that the picture they were working on was a hotbed of discontent.

"Brandon," Elaine began after a moment's hesitation, "I want to keep us private. I don't want anyone to know about us yet."

"Because of your father?" Brandon asked.

"That's part of it. I also prefer my private life and my public life to be separate."

"I'm glad, because I like to live that way."

"Brandon?"

Brandon didn't reply, but continued to gaze at her.

"Have you noticed any 'discontent' on the set?" she asked.

"At the beginning, but not now."

"I just wanted to make sure. Brandon . . . do you like working with John Hart?"

"I like working with you," he replied as his eyes locked with hers.

"Brandon, talk to me," she reiterated.

"He's all right; he knows his stuff."

"But?"

"But nothing. Everything's been routine. There haven't been any creative problems for him to solve. He's doing everything by the book."

Brandon saw how troubled she was, and knew that there was little he could say to ease her mind. He had been very much aware of the antagonism between her and the director, and had sensed that it would be something that stayed on throughout the picture. "Can we drop the shop talk?" he asked gently.

Elaine nodded, but a moment later a frown once again changed her expression.

"Lanie, is anything else bothering you?"

"Yes," she admitted, but the sadness in her voice was denied by the impish smile she couldn't quite hide.

"And?"

"I haven't been kissed in a half hour."

"Really? Well, all you have to do is get off your—ah, chair, and come over here."

"Really?" she mimicked, "and I thought chivalry was dead."

"No, just resting from a hectic day," he declared with a grin.

"Oh!" Elaine exclaimed, picking up her napkin and flinging it at him.

"And I love you, too," he replied ducking the poorly aimed shot. "Now, are you coming over here or not?"

Shaking her head, Elaine rose from her chair and slowly walked to him. When she was at his side, she bent seductively and lowered her lips to his. She felt both his hands on her back and she moved her arm carefully until her fingers touched the cold water pitcher. Moving gracefully, Elaine withdrew from his embrace and dumped the contents of the pitcher on his head.

"Chauvinist!" she declared, unable to hold back her laughter at the sight of his drenched head.

"I'll get you," he threatened, rising menacingly.

"I know," Elaine said as she ran out of the dining room, a bare three feet ahead of him.

Elaine bent low in the saddle, her cheek almost resting against the damp neck of the quarter horse as she urged it to move faster. The wind in her face and the powerful, surging strides of the horse combined to give her a sense of oneness with the land around her, the beauty of being a part of it all.

She twisted her neck to look back, and smiled at the scene behind her. Brandon was ten feet back and catching up, with Cynthia almost at his horse's tail. Far behind them, bouncing like a madman while he tried to keep his seat, was Simon Arnold, the novice who had said he could ride.

Elaine reined in her gelding as she passed the entrance to the corral. Sitting back in the saddle, she drew the reins tight in a forced stop. Then she spun the horse about and waited until the other three had joined her.

"Not bad," Brandon said with a smile as he leaned across his horse to kiss her lightly.

"You're not bad for a city boy, either," Elaine rejoined.

"He beat me, didn't he?" Cindy demanded as she reached them.

Then all three watched Simon plod his way to them, and each, to their credit, tried not to laugh.

"I told you I could ride," he said proudly.

"I think 'bounce' would be a better word," Brandon stated.

"I'm just a little out of practice," said the playwright.

"When was the last time you went riding?" Cindy asked.

"About thirty years ago," he admitted.

"Thirty . . . Simon, you're only thirty-two," Cindy said in a puzzled tone.

"The last time I rode a horse was when I was two. My mother put me on a pony at the fair. I fell off and wouldn't ever go on again," he admitted with a shamefaced grin that made everyone laugh.

"In that case," Elaine said when she stopped laughing, "I'd suggest a long, hot bath, if you expect to be able to walk tomorrow."

"I'm in good shape," Simon protested. "Aren't I?" he asked Cindy.

Blushing, Cindy nodded. "But the bath is still a good idea," Cindy replied without looking at either Brandon or Elaine. "Come on, cowboy," she added as she dismounted and began to lead her horse toward the stable.

"Giddyap," Simon chanted, urging his horse after Cindy's.

Elaine gazed at Brandon, and they both smiled. "He'll be very sore after taking that pounding."

"Maybe it'll teach him a lesson," Brandon said with a knowing nod of his head. For his part, Brandon had enjoyed the ride and the feeling of being away from the real world.

"You ride nicely," Elaine said as she dismounted.

"Thank you," Brandon replied, joining her on the

ground. Side by side, they walked toward the stable. "I used to ride on weekends upstate."

"Used to?" Elaine queried.

"When I wasn't in a play. But when I am, I ride in Central Park. It makes me feel good to sit on a horse; it takes me away from reality."

"That's as good a reason as any."

"Lanie, I've really enjoyed myself."

"So have I. It's been very nice," she told him. At the stable they unsaddled their horses, brushed them down and then let them loose in the corral. With that done, Elaine and Brandon followed Cindy and Simon, who had finished a few moments before them, to the house.

"I am in desperate need of a bath," Elaine stated. She wrinkled her nose in emphasis to her words and at the heady scent floating from her—a scent that was a combination of horse, hay and her own perspiration.

"I agree," Brandon added.

"Oh! And I suppose you think you smell macho?" she chided.

Brandon laughed and shook his head. "No, I meant I needed to clean up also, but I'll take a shower."

"Good ride?" Lawrence Rodman asked them.

"Great," Elaine replied. "I'm going to take a bath. I'll call when the bathroom's free," she told Brandon as she entered the house, leaving him and her father together.

"I guess this is the point when we're supposed to feel each other out," Lawrence said as he gazed steadily into Brandon's eyes.

"Ask away," Brandon offered.

Lawrence smiled, then his eyes flicked past Brandon's shoulder. He shook his head quickly. "Later, perhaps,"

he said mysteriously. Smiling, Lawrence clapped Brandon
on the back. "When we talk, I won't want any interrup-
tions," he added as he stepped down from the porch and
walked toward a car that was just pulling into the drive.

Brandon watched him for a moment, and saw the
white-haired man take a large envelope from the driver.
Shrugging his shoulders, Brandon went into the house and
up the central staircase to his room, where he undressed,
put on a robe and waited for one of the two bathrooms to
become vacant.

Lying in the warm water of the bath, Elaine rested her
head on its porcelain edge and closed her eyes as the
heated water worked its magic on her muscles. Since their
arrival late yesterday, everything had gone nicely. She
wanted to forget the movie and the problems that were
plaguing it and just enjoy herself.

Although they had reached the ranch later than they'd
planned, it was wonderful to first see it in the twilight. The
main house was a two-story brick-and-wood building that
sat regally amid a small grove of trees. Two stables and a
large barn sat a hundred feet behind the house and Jamie
Langely's house was a quarter of a mile down the road.
Jamie had been foreman of the ranch since her father had
purchased it twelve years ago. He was also the man who'd
taught her to ride and even to fly the ranch's helicopter
during her many summer-long stays.

Across the short road from Jamie's house was the
bunkhouse, for those hands who were single or preferred
to live on the ranch during the week.

"Fantastic," Simon had whispered from the backseat.

At the long and winding entrance to the ranch, Elaine

had asked Brandon to stop the car. When he did, she turned to him, her smile one of apology.

"I think we'd better talk now, before we get there."

"Yes?" Brandon asked.

She had glanced nervously at Brandon, and then had spoken in a low voice. "I . . . we'll be in separate bedrooms," she'd whispered.

Brandon had arched his eyebrows at this, but he remained silent.

"My father is a bit old-fashioned. . . . Besides," she said proudly, when he'd favored her with a sardonic smile, "I like him like that!"

"Then why are you so nervous about it?" Brandon had asked.

"I'm not!" Elaine had retorted, turning to the backseat and staring defiantly at Cindy and Simon. "That goes for the two of you as well!"

"I already told Simon," Cynthia said with a smile.

"Can we go on now?" Brandon had asked.

Elaine had nodded, averting her eyes from his half-taunting smile.

Elaine sighed as she added more hot water, listening to the sound echo in the bathroom. Dinner last night had been a relaxing time, and her father had been a genial host, never prying into their relationships but always keeping the pace of the conversation flowing. After eating, they'd gone into the large, rustic living room to sit before the roaring fire, drink a light, white wine and listen to music. By eleven, everyone had been showing signs of sleepiness, and Lawrence had suggested they adjourn to their rooms.

Cindy and Simon had gone up first, and after Elaine had

kissed her father good night, she and Brandon had followed. It had been strange to kiss Brandon good night at the door to her old bedroom, but it felt right, too.

She had lain awake for a time, thinking about her father and Brandon, and had fallen asleep hoping that they would like each other.

A sharp knock on the bathroom door pulled Elaine from her thoughts. "Yes?"

"Lanie, there's a call for you. It's Jason Heller," her father informed her.

What now? she wondered. "I'll be right there," she told her father. Rising quickly, Elaine let the water cascade from her body before she stepped out of the tub and wrapped herself in a towel. She slipped on her robe and left the bathroom, stopping at Brandon's door.

"Bathroom's free," she shouted. Then she walked to her room to pick up the phone, wondering what her assistant producer wanted. *Let it be nothing important,* she prayed. She wanted, and needed, the next days with Brandon.

"Jason?" she asked when she picked up the receiver.

"Elaine, I'm sorry to bother you but . . ."

"What's wrong?"

"Look," Jason began. Elaine heard the hesitation in his voice, but rather than prod him, she waited, her intuition warning her to hold back. "I know that John Hart has certain rights as director, but I think he's overstepping them."

"Jason, please tell me what's going on," Elaine said, her hand tightening on the receiver.

"Well, Lorraine Adams's agent called today. She won't be working on the picture."

"Why?" Elaine closed her eyes, a picture of Lorraine Adams coming to mind. Lorraine, a rising young starlet, had a minor but important role in the movie.

"The agent wouldn't say. Just that she couldn't fulfill her commitment to *Distant Worlds*."

"I see." Elaine didn't, but it was not an unusual occurrence. But Lorraine had been very excited about doing this picture. "And?"

"And Hart notified me an hour ago that he had hired Suzanne Roland as Lorraine's replacement."

"He what? He has no right!"

"I'm sorry, Miss Rodman, but he's already told her agent to have her on the set Tuesday morning."

"We'll see about that," Elaine whispered, more to herself than to Jason. "I hope that's all he's done."

"Not quite," Jason replied softly.

"What else?" Elaine asked, a sinking sensation in the pit of her stomach.

"He's changed the shooting location for one of the scenes and informed me that there will be script changes to go with it."

"No there won't!" Elaine snapped. "All right, Jason, I'll be there in . . ." Elaine paused to estimate how long it would take her to reach the location. If she left after dinner, she'd be there by midnight. She could be up early and face Hart in the morning, before the director went any further. "Have my motel room available by midnight. I'll talk to you when I get in."

"No problem," replied Jason, relief evident in his voice.

"And, thank you Jason," she added just before she hung up.

Elaine sat deep in thought for several moments after hanging up the phone. Hart's presumptuousness angered her, but she forced back the emotion and she began to plan her countermoves.

She would speak to Lorraine's agent first, and find out why Lorraine had left the picture. There was still a matter of her contract. Elaine wondered why Hart would hire Suzanne Roland to replace Lorraine. Lorraine was an excellent actress, but Suzanne, despite her extraordinary beauty, couldn't act.

But even more important were the location and script changes. That was not only unacceptable, it was prohibited by Simon Arnold's contract, which stated that he must agree to any changes.

Elaine galvanized herself into action. She dressed and went down to her father's library to call David Leaser at home. But when she reached the Leasers' housekeeper, she was informed that David and his wife had gone away for the weekend. She wouldn't be able to reach him until tomorrow, after lunch.

Now the real function of a producer reaffirmed itself in her mind. She knew that tomorrow would be yet another test, and one that she must handle alone and handle properly.

"Trouble?" Lawrence Rodman asked, stepping into the library.

Elaine turned to face her father. "Maybe. I have to leave after dinner."

"Being a producer has its bad points."

"And its good ones, too. You taught me that," Elaine responded with a smile.

"Want to talk about it?" he asked.

"I really don't know all the details," she began, then she slowly nodded her head and told him what Jason had reported.

"I take it this has been happening from the start?"

"He resents my taking over from Tom Sellert."

"And also that you're my daughter?" he asked wisely.

"It has certain—"

"Stigmas," Lawrence finished for her.

"I was going to say 'advantages and disadvantages,'" Elaine said uncomfortably.

"Same difference. Lanie, you know the truth about how you got the job. That's all that should matter to you. Now, what are you planning to do about Hart?"

"I'm going to veto what he's done."

"How about making a compromise?"

"Why? He's trying to get away with whatever he can," she stated, refusing to soften her stand.

"What's more important, the script and location changes, or the actress?"

"I won't know until I've seen the changes."

"Compromise, Lanie. Let him have the lesser of the two evils. Think about it," he advised.

"I will," Elaine promised. "About Brandon and . . ."

"Will they be staying?"

"They deserve their time off. Would you mind?" she asked.

"Not if they don't. I haven't seen Cindy in a while, and both Brandon and Simon seem like nice men."

"Thank you, Daddy."

"Lanie, is it getting serious between you and Brandon?" Lawrence asked, his eyes searching her face openly.

"I think so," she whispered.

"So do I," Lawrence said with a knowing smile. "Now, you'd better let our guests know that you're leaving. I'll see you at dinner."

Elaine nodded, then kissed her father's cheek tenderly. "Thank you, Daddy."

When she left the library, Lawrence Rodman sat in the chair his daughter had just vacated and opened the top drawer of his desk. He took out the large manila envelope that had been delivered a half hour before and slit the sealed lip.

Carefully, he withdrew the neatly typed papers and scanned them. A moment later only a bomb could have distracted him as he read one of the most informative, interesting and revealing pieces of information he'd seen in years, while, on the floor above him, Elaine was telling Brandon that she had to leave for Death Valley after dinner.

"I'll go with you," Brandon said quickly.

Elaine shook her head emphatically. "No. This is part of my job. I want you to relax and enjoy tomorrow. You've got a hard week ahead of you."

"Oh?" he snapped, his temper blazing at her words. "Or is it just that you don't want anyone to know about us?"

"That's not fair," Elaine retorted, stung by his words.

"It wasn't meant to be."

"Brandon, don't make this anymore difficult than it already is. I told you that what is between us personally should stay that way. I have a job to do, and if the rest of the cast and crew knew about us, it would make it harder, if not impossible."

Brandon looked at her for a long moment. "I'm sorry," he said as his hands wove around her waist and drew her to him. "I'm just disappointed at losing this time with you."

"So am—" But he cut off her words with his lips, as he kissed her deeply, showing her the way he felt with his mouth, hands and body.

When they drew apart, their eyes said more to each other than any words could.

"Call me if you need my help," he whispered.

"I will," she promised.

At eight o'clock, Elaine got behind the wheel of Brandon's rental car and waved good-bye to the others. Brandon had insisted she take his car, since the studio had rented it for him anyway. Before she left the house, she had arranged for another car to be delivered to the ranch the next day.

When the car pulled out of the drive, Cynthia and Simon walked toward the corral, their arms around each other's waists.

"They seem to be very much in love," Lawrence said to Brandon.

"I can't speak for Cindy, but I know Simon was lost the first time he met Cindy."

"He's a nice man. A bit different from most of today's scriptwriters. He reminds me of the writers I worked with in the beginning—very serious people."

Brandon paused to gaze intently at Larry Rodman for a moment. "He is."

"That's good, because Cindy is a serious person also. I've known her since she was two, and she's almost as close to me as Lanie is."

Brandon laughed.

"Am I amusing you?" Lawrence asked.

"No, sir," Brandon replied. "It's just that I think you want to bring up something else and you're trying to figure out how to do it."

Lawrence stared at him and then nodded his head, a grin on his lips. "You're astute. But I am concerned about Cynthia, as well."

"Simon isn't one to take another person's emotions and feelings lightly."

"And you?"

"Neither am I," Brandon stated calmly.

"You seem like a man who is not overly reticent. Why don't we go inside and talk?"

Brandon followed Larry Rodman into the library, sat down next to him on the leather couch and waited for him to begin.

"Elaine is very important to me," he said.

"She is to me, also," Brandon cut in.

"Lanie's not like the usual people you meet in the film business, and . . . I don't want to see her hurt," Lawrence said, his eyes locking with Brandon's.

"And you think I'm like the others in the industry? Are you saying you want me out of her life?" Brandon asked, anger beginning to build.

"No. I'm simply telling you that I love my daughter, and I'll do whatever is necessary to protect her from being hurt."

Brandon had first thought that Rodman was trying to tell him to leave his daughter alone, but now he wasn't sure. He was caught between anger and curiosity and he waited to see what her father would say next.

"Have you told her about yourself?" Lawrence asked.

"Myself?" he questioned in a low voice.

Lawrence Rodman rose gracefully to his feet, drawing

himself to his full height. He smiled charmingly at Brandon, then went to his desk. He picked up the stack of neatly typed pages and turned back to Brandon.

"Yes, yourself. Brandon Winslow Michaels the third. Born in Boston, graduated summa cum laude from Boston University with a degree in computer science. Founded Mi-Tech, Inc.; investments and acquisitions in many and diverse areas."

Brandon listened to Lawrence Rodman reading what he'd thought to be his well-hidden life history and felt a chill race along his back. Suddenly he was on his feet, staring at the older man.

"How did you find out?" he demanded.

"Brandon, as you should know, when you have the financial resources nothing is impossible."

"All right, Mr. Rodman, what's your point?"

"That's what I'm trying to find out."

"My financial background has nothing to do with my feelings for your daughter."

"Brandon, what concerns me is that you have a propensity for doing many things. You seem to get bored with one thing and go on to another. Will that happen with Elaine?"

"First of all, I don't get bored easily. But when there aren't any more challenges, when I've done everything I can and proven that I do it well, I move on to what piques my interest next." Brandon spoke in a tight voice. His eyes held Lawrence Rodman's without blinking. "That's the way I am, professionally. I have also found that acting is a never-ending challenge. That every role holds something for me to reach for. That's why I've settled into acting. As far as your daughter is concerned, what happens between us is exactly that, between us."

Before Brandon had finished his heated statement, he saw the tension leave Lawrence's face and a smile etch its way onto his features.

"Thank you," Elaine's father said, catching Brandon completely off guard.

"Excuse me?"

"For being honest. You're wrong, though, in thinking that what happens between Lanie and yourself is only your business, because I'm her father and she's *my* business, but you're right, also."

"Now I understand where she gets it," Brandon muttered.

"Gets what?"

"Everything. She's her father's daughter."

"Again, I thank you for the compliment. Now that we've settled that, would you care for a drink?"

Settled what? Brandon wanted to ask, but didn't. He liked Elaine's father, and their talk hadn't changed that. "Fine."

Lawrence poured two glasses of brandy and turned back to Brandon as if nothing had happened, beginning to ask him questions.

"Now, tell me what you think is happening on the film. I've been rather disturbed by what I've heard . . ."

Chapter 9

THE SUN HAD BEEN UP FOR AN HOUR WHEN ELAINE topped the rise of the dirt road and stopped the car. Below her, spread out in a magnificent panorama, was the sand and rock valley that would be the first location shoot of *Distant Worlds*. Like a wagon train of old, RVs, trailers, tractor trailers, and tents were set up in a circle.

Elaine gazed at the scene below her and mentally ticked off each vehicle and its purpose, from the mobile film laboratory next to the equipment trailers to the makeup and costume trailers to the portable kitchen and toilets. At the edge of the trailers were five RVs that would be used as dressing rooms and offices. All in all, everything seemed ready.

"Hart's car is by the offices," Jason said as he pointed to a low-slung Jaguar parked next to the third RV.

Elaine nodded and pressed down on the accelerator. A

few minutes later she pulled in next to Hart's car and shut off the engine.

"Wait out here," Elaine told Jason. Taking a deep breath, Elaine knocked on the door with Hart's name on it. She heard him call out, opened the door and stepped up into the RV.

"My goodness, Miss Producer, this is a surprise," Hart said without leaving his chair.

"But not an unexpected one?"

"You're not due here until tomorrow. Of course it's unexpected. Coffee?" he asked, gesturing toward a steaming pot.

"No. Talk," she replied as she sat down across from him. "I understand you've made a few changes."

"Yes."

"Why?"

"Because you were unavailable and, as the director, I have the right."

"John, I don't know why you're fighting me so hard, but we both know what our rights and responsibilities are on this film. Why did Lorraine quit?"

"What difference does it make? She's gone."

"It makes a lot of difference. She's a damned good actress."

"And Suzanne Rolands isn't?"

"You know the answer to that," Elaine whispered.

"No, I don't. Why don't you tell me?" the director demanded harshly.

"The studio's choice for the part was Lorraine Adams."

"But she's gone and, as the director, I made a decision on her replacement, which is within my realm of responsibility."

"To recommend someone to me, the producer, for the part is your responsibility—not to hire someone on your own!"

"What's wrong? Do you think I'm trying to undermine your authority? How could I? Your daddy would have me blacklisted."

Rage flared briefly at his words, but Elaine forced it back. "The only thing that will get you blacklisted is your attitude. Dammit, Hart, I'm trying to do a good job."

"Then do your job and let me do mine!" Hart shouted, slamming his fist on the table between them. "Now, if there's nothing further?"

Elaine took a long, slow breath before she spoke. "We have another matter to discuss."

Hart sighed exasperatedly. "We haven't even begun to work and you're trying to interfere with everything I've done."

"Not to interfere, to help and work with you. I understand you've changed the location and script for one of the scenes."

"That's right. So?" he challenged.

"I want to see the script, and the locale. Then Simon Arnold must also."

"This is ridiculous. How am I supposed to direct a picture I have no control over?"

"The way it should be directed. If not, Mr. Director, quit!" Elaine said in a voice so low it could be barely heard.

Hart stiffened, and his face took on an ugly expression. "You'd like that, wouldn't you? Sorry, lady, you're not going to chop my head off the way you did Sellert's."

"He chopped his own head off. The script?" she asked,

her voice level, not allowing him to see her anger and frustration.

Hart moved a pile of papers around, extracted several loose sheets and flung them at her with a sneer. "Now, if you'll excuse me, I'm very busy."

Elaine stood with the script pages in her hand. "I want to see the location."

"Tell your boy wonder to take you there."

Elaine knew he was referring to Jason. "All right. I want to meet with you after lunch. I wouldn't want to spoil your appetite before then. Be in my trailer at one," she ordered, leaving before Hart could say anything else.

Outside, Elaine paused to regroup her emotions. The meeting had lasted no more than seven minutes, but she was as tired as if she'd run ten miles.

"Are you okay?" Jason asked.

"Fine. Do you know where the new location is?"

"About a mile from here."

"All right. Drive me there, will you?" she asked as she moved to the passenger side of the car, got in and began to read the changes Hart had made.

As the sounds of the car engine receded, John Hart looked out the window at the trail of dust raised by the wheels. "You can come out now," he called.

The door to the rear room of the RV opened, and a dark man of medium height came out.

"She took the bait?" he asked.

"I told you she would. Any bets about what she says this afternoon?"

"No bets."

"Good. You'll have your revenge soon enough."

"You're sure about the other thing?" he asked the director.

"Would I have gone through the hassle of getting Lorraine off the picture if I wasn't sure?"

"I'm counting on that. Suzanne knows her part? She knows what's expected of her?"

"She knows. After all, this will make her a star, won't it?" Hart asked sarcastically. Both men laughed, exchanging knowing looks.

When Elaine finally picked up her room key at the lavish, sprawling resort motel situated in the gently rolling hills on the edge of Death Valley, she took a shower and changed into a comfortable, baggy jogging suit.

While she toweled dry her hair she stood at her window watching the spectacular desert sunset, the myriad striking colors painting the wasteland of Death Valley like an artist's palette.

Elaine gazed at the beauty before her, sighing with relief that this wearying day was almost over. It had been a day filled with aggravation, dead ends, and an unpleasant decision she had been forced to make.

When she and Jason had gone to the location, after she had read the script changes, Elaine knew they couldn't be permitted to go through. The changes altered the basic concept of the screenplay and were badly written to boot, which made the location change pointless.

After returning to the equipment location, she'd gone to the RV that was her office to find that the phones had been set up. She called Lorraine's agent and demanded to know why Lorraine had quit the film. He'd been honest, telling Elaine that his client and the director had had insoluble differences.

When Elaine tried to talk him into asking her to reconsider, the agent had added that another reason for Lorraine's leaving the film was the trouble and tension on the set.

Elaine had brought up her contract, as a minor threat, but the agent had dismissed it out of hand, citing union regulations regarding illness. It was then that Elaine had accepted this setback.

When she'd met with Hart that afternoon she'd chosen the only path she felt comfortable with. She didn't want to fight with him, but she couldn't give in completely.

"I'll approve Suzanne Roland's contract," she'd told him.

"That's wise," he'd said unemotionally.

"But the script and locale changes will not be approved. I'm sorry, but that's my decision."

"I see," Hart had said as he stared at her with his small gray eyes. Then he shook his head slowly. "I should have expected that. Very well, we'll go back to the original script." Still shaking his head, Hart had left the RV.

Elaine, for her part, had been surprised at the ease with which Hart had accepted her decision. Then she put the matter out of her mind and began to go over the inventory lists that Chick Uldridge had given her a half hour before.

Now, Elaine gazed out at the rapidly darkening landscape and found herself wishing that Brandon had been with her today. She knew that she could have spoken to him, told him her problems, and that he would have helped her work them out. It was then that Elaine realized just how much Brandon was becoming a part of her life.

A gentle knock on the motel room's door pulled Elaine from her thoughts and her contemplation of the fading sunset. She went to the door and opened it. Her breath caught and a smile lit her face.

"Hello, stranger," Brandon whispered.

"Hello." Elaine breathed the word rather than speaking it. Stepping back, she motioned for Brandon to come in. When the door was closed she went eagerly into his arms, kissing him ardently, as if she hadn't seen him in weeks.

The tension of the day drained magically away now that she was in his arms, as did the sluggishness of her blood, which exploded in reaction to his kiss. A long minute later they drew apart.

"Miss me?" Brandon asked.

"Should I have?"

"I'd like to think you did."

"No one's stopping you from your thoughts," she teased.

"You are. I can't think when you're in my arms."

"Who told you to think?" she replied, her voice husky as she kissed him passionately.

This time when they parted their chests were straining powerfully and their eyes drank of each other's faces, until a strange gurgling noise rose between them. Elaine's cheeks turned crimson in response, and Brandon laughed.

"It's not funny!" she stated.

"When did you last eat?" Brandon asked.

Elaine didn't look at him. "It was a crazy day. I had some toast and coffee this morning . . ."

"I can't let you out of my sight for a day, can I? It's a good thing I got here when I did."

"Oh, really?"

"Yes, really," he said as another knock sounded on the door.

Elaine started to answer it, but Brandon stopped her with a hand on her arm. "Allow me."

"Bran . . ." she began.

"Stop being so frightened that someone will find out our *secret!*" he said tersely.

Elaine froze, but forced herself to stay calm. He was right; she couldn't continue to be on guard so much. As Brandon reached for the door she remembered how badly she had wanted him to be there this afternoon, and she began to relax.

When he opened the door she stared at the room-service waiter standing beside his cart. A few minutes later, the man had gone, and Brandon motioned her to the table.

"As I was saying before we were interrupted," Brandon began as he sat down across from her, "it's a good thing I got here when I did. Who knows, you might have starved to death."

"Brandon," Elaine said as she drank in the handsomeness of his face and felt the rapid beating of her heart, "I did miss you, and I do love you."

"I know," Brandon replied with a wink. "Eat," he ordered with a wave of his hand.

"Yes, sir!"

They ate the meal in silence, content to be together, without the need for further talk. They finished their food and Elaine poured the coffee.

"How are the two lovebirds?" she asked.

"They're fine. When we got up here, they brought their bags to their rooms and Simon informed me that there was no emergency in the world that would be allowed to disturb him. The last I saw of him was when he disappeared into Cindy's room."

"Ah, true love . . ."

"I think it is," Brandon said seriously.

"They're a good pair."

"But they're not what concerns me at the moment," Brandon said. He had waited until he felt the time was right and now he asked, "What happened today?"

She told him everything that had happened and what she'd done about it. She was surprised at how easy it was to speak to Brandon. When she finished she waited for his response.

"You're a smart producer. I think you took the only course possible," he said honestly. But what he didn't voice was his concern about why Lorraine had left the film. Something didn't seem quite right.

"Brandon?"

"Yes?" he asked, aware of the change in her voice.

"It's getting late."

"I know," he whispered. Then he rose and walked over to her. "Very late," he added.

They came together and Elaine's breasts, bare beneath a cotton jogging top, were crushed against his muscular chest. Desire welled up within her, and her passion turned her blood into a molten river.

Then she was on the bed and her clothing was gone. Brandon stood above her, naked as she, his green eyes caressing her body, letting her read his love and desire.

Brandon gazed upon her beauty, and his chest tightened. Then he was on the bed with her. He tasted the sweetness of her lips, and as he did, a shiver ran the length of his body. The softness of her breasts against him, the hardness of her nipples and the tantalizing heated silk of her skin all affected him deeply.

As his lips explored the delicate curve of her neck he felt her hands on his shoulders, pushing him away.

Their eyes locked for a moment before Brandon sighed and gave in to her urgings. Then he was on his back, with Elaine cradled in one arm, her lips trailing a heated path along his neck.

Elaine inhaled his heady, powerful male scent as her lips moved tantalizingly over him. Like a butterfly fluttering over a field of flowers, her lips moved along the tender skin of his chest.

Elaine unraveled the bonds that had held her passion in check, and gave herself over to the touch, taste and feel of the man she loved. The smooth rippling of his muscles beneath her lips sent the fires within her flaming higher.

Weaving through the mat of hair on his chest, kissing and biting gently, Elaine journeyed along his body. Her senses were approaching the boiling point, but she couldn't quench her desire to touch and taste every inch of him.

Brandon forced his aching body to be still. The desire Lanie created was like a bomb building slowly, maddeningly, to the point of explosion. Her lips were everywhere, driving him wild with their lightest touch. Her hands, too, moved in a smoothly blending tattoo that she disrupted only to be continued with her wandering, soft lips.

Brandon was aware of a thousand different sensations and realized that this was more than just a heightening of physical desire. This was a truly beautiful giving that suddenly made him aware of the full extent of his love for her.

Elaine sensed Brandon's tension building beneath her

ministrations, as every part of his body called to her. The tight, smooth skin of his thighs was like polished velvet beneath her fingertips. The myriad sensations caused by his skin against hers as she moved along his length sent her passions soaring to the farthest reaches of her existence as she felt his body grow even more heated beneath her touch. He was on fire, calling to her with silent desire.

Suddenly his hands were on her shoulders, tightening, urging, until she slid upward along his body, returning to his mouth to take in the heated thrust of his tongue. Her body, too, burned feverishly, and her mind was a blank except for the knowledge of the man she was with.

Slowly, retaining only the barest grasp of reality, Elaine moved from Brandon's chest, pulling him onto her. Her legs wrapped around him and her mouth was covered by his as she guided him into her.

With a slow, burning thrust, he filled her, making Elaine cry out in pleasure, her fingers turning to claws digging into the resilient skin of his back.

"Love me!" she cried in his ear as her body arched to meet his, picking up his rhythm immediately and blending with his every movement.

Brandon's senses were attacked on every level as he strove to follow Elaine's husky plea. "I do," he whispered. He drew her tighter to him and let himself be surrounded by the almost unbearable warmth of her entire being. The caress of her breath on his shoulder and the scent of her hair in his nose sent his mind reeling.

The touch of his chest against her nipples and the force of his love within her sent waves of ecstasy streaking through her. Brandon carried Elaine forward, faster and faster, until she could only hold on to him in desperation.

His strong hands were cupping her derriere, making her a willing prisoner as he pressed her tighter against him. Every fiber of her being responded totally, commanded by the sheer power and force of her lover.

As he grew harder and his thrusts deepened within her, Elaine's muscles contracted and an explosion was released deep within her very soul. Elaine's loud moan filled the air, echoed by Brandon's, until they were silenced by the joining of their lips.

They stayed together, neither moving, both afraid to part and break the bond that had formed between them in so earthshaking a way.

They were both trembling from the intensity of their lovemaking, and from the new knowledge of the magnitude and strength of their love for each other.

Slowly they moved apart, only to come together again, side by side, secure and comfortable within each other's arms. The last thing she saw before she fell asleep was the warm glow of his green eyes upon her face.

The staccato sound of a beeping alarm dragged her up through the layers of sleep. She opened her eyes and began to sit up when the sound abruptly stopped.

"What?" she asked.

"It's almost morning. I have to go," Brandon told her as he turned on a light and pressed a button on his watch.

Blinking away the flickering afterimages from the light, Elaine gazed at Brandon's face and sleep-tousled hair.

"Good morning," she whispered.

"It is." Brandon smiled and leaned over to kiss her. He felt wonderful, as if he'd slept for a week. "But my call is at five, and I have to be ready. Besides," he added with a smile, "if I don't leave now, someone will see me coming out of your room."

"Brandon, please," Elaine whispered, hurt and wishing the situation could be different.

"It's all right," he said quickly when he saw the effect of his words on her face. "Lanie, I'm sorry. I was just teasing."

"It has to be this way. You must understand that," she said, as if she hadn't heard him.

"I'm trying, dammit, I *am* trying, but it's hard. I don't like sneaking around, hiding from other people for no good reason."

"You're wrong. There are very good reasons," Elaine said in open challenge.

Brandon paused for a moment, then shook his head slowly as he banished the unreasonable anger that had surged so quickly and so needlessly. "I know," he replied. "And, perhaps for the first time, I do understand why."

It was true, Brandon realized suddenly, as the past few days' events fell into place. Gathering Elaine into his arms, he held her tightly. After what he had learned from Elaine's father and what Elaine had told him last night, he knew that her situation was precarious, and that being the daughter of a famous movie producer was a cross she had to not only bear, but rise above. Being involved, publicly, with the film's star would be the last thing that would help her.

He kissed her lightly and squeezed her to him. "It'll all work out," he said.

"I hope so," she whispered against his cheek. "Go!" she ordered, drawing away from him.

"Yes, ma'am," he replied, releasing her and rising in a graceful movement that took her breath away.

Elaine lay back down, drawing the sheet up to her neck as Brandon dressed. When he was finished he came back to the side of the bed and kissed her closed eyelids.

"Mmmmm," Elaine breathed.

"Want me to stay?" Brandon asked.

Elaine opened her eyes and stared directly into his before she spoke. "Forever."

"Let's work on it," Brandon replied. Then, with a lopsided grin, he winked at her. "See you on location, boss lady."

"And don't forget that," Elaine quipped as Brandon stepped through the door and closed it behind him.

Elaine stayed in bed for a few more minutes after he'd gone, and then forced her body into action. Looking outside, she saw it was still dark, but she knew that the sun would start to rise just about the time the actors were made-up for the first scene of the day.

The reality of making a movie was a far cry from what the public believed it to be. When you worked on a movie you were usually out of bed between three-thirty and four o'clock, and at the studio, or on the location, no later than 5:00 A.M. That, plus the fact that when working, a film person rarely got to bed after ten at night. *No,* Elaine thought, *making movies was not what people believed.*

Turning on the shower and stepping into the stall, Elaine washed away both the sleep and the effect of rising early, as she prepared herself for the craziness of the filming today and in the days to come.

As Brandon closed the door of Elaine's room, he looked

around the deserted walkway, then started toward his room. Across the way, in the opposite wing of the motel, two men stared out their window at him. When Brandon was out of sight, the bearded man turned on a light.

"As I said. It's a fact."

The swarthy man nodded, and then he smiled. "So it is."

Chapter 10

A LOUD KNOCK DREW ELAINE FROM THE PAPERS SHE WAS looking over. "Come in," she responded.

Chick Uldridge opened the door and stepped into Elaine's field office.

"More problems?" she asked. From the expression on his face, she knew the answer. For every day of the last two weeks there had been one problem or another, some minor, some big. The problems ran anywhere from spoiled food to lost negatives, and nothing she had done had helped stop the problems.

"The equipment trailer was broken into again last night. All the unexposed film was stolen, except for what was in the cameras. We have to wait for more film to be delivered before we can start work today."

"What were the guards doing?" she demanded, anger making her voice sharp.

"I can't say. There were three men on duty, just as you requested, but they swore they didn't hear a thing."

"Wonderful. Two weeks on location and we're behind four days and ten thousand dollars over budget. Chick, it's got to stop."

"I know," the stage manager said, shaking his head. He was as upset as Elaine, possibly more so because the equipment was his primary responsibility. And he still hadn't gotten over the fire at the studio. "But I have an idea."

"Anything! Just tell me before I speak to Leaser. He's going to want an explanation."

"I'd like to move into your office—without anyone knowing. I want to spend a few nights here and see what's going on."

Elaine looked at him for a moment, deep in thought. Chick was a big, burly man, and she knew he prided himself on his work and his ability to get the job done. But with all that was happening, Elaine wondered if it might be too dangerous.

"We don't know who or how many people are involved . . ."

"That's what I want to find out. I won't do anything foolish; I just want to see them." Chick had read his boss's thoughts, and knew exactly what to say.

"All right," Elaine agreed. "But you be careful. I'll make sure there's food left here for you."

"No," he said quickly. "I'll take care of it. I don't want anyone to know."

"Just be careful," she told him again as he left. Then she picked up the phone, knowing she couldn't put off her call to David any longer—he had called yesterday while she was out, and had left a message for Elaine to call him in the morning.

When she hung up her face was set in grim lines of determination. The chairman of the board wanted to see her first thing tomorrow morning—with all the footage shot to date. She would have to take a private plane to Los Angeles early in the morning and explain the delays to him in person. "Dammit all, anyway!" she shouted to the empty RV.

"And I think that stinks!" declared Suzanne Roland when she finished telling her little story. She glanced around the table at the various expressions on everyone's faces.

"What makes you so sure about that?" asked one of the extras, who was supposed to be in the scene shot today. A scene that was not going to be shot until they got more film.

"Because I heard it from a good source," the starlet stated.

"Look, everyone knows that this picture is Leaser's baby, and that Tom Sellert and Leaser didn't see eye to eye about it. That's why he's gone," said the woman in charge of continuity, who made sure every scene followed the script and that all the props were in the right places so that scenes that were reshot from different angles looked exactly the same as the original. That included everything from the amount of liquid in a glass to the hand in which an actor had held a cigarette in the previous take.

"Not true," Suzanne replied adamantly. "Rodman played politics and her father called in favors from Leaser. That's why!"

Brandon had sat quietly as everyone debated the rights and wrongs of the film's production. But he had heard a defensiveness in Suzanne's voice that warranted further consideration.

"Suzanne," Brandon said in a low voice that captured the attention of everyone at the table. "For someone who joined the picture as late as you did, it seems a bit strange for you to be so well informed."

Brandon watched her face change, her eyes narrowing slightly as she moistened her full lips with her tongue. When she spoke, her voice was throatier, too. "That's where you're wrong," she said. "I was offered this part before Lorraine Adams was even thought of!"

"Really?" Brandon asked, widening his eyes at this piece of information.

"Yes. But when little Miss Rodman got Sellert dumped, I lost the part. *She* wanted Lorraine Adams, and David Leaser let her drop me."

"All right, folks. Sorry to interrupt this chitchat, but the film's here, so we can go to work," Jason Heller announced, stopping at their table.

"I guess that means makeup again?" Brandon said with a grin.

"Yup," Jason agreed. Then he turned to Suzanne. "You, too."

"I'm not in this scene."

"Hart's decided to shoot two scenes. He'll work with Brandon's scene and the AD will handle yours. He wants to get back on schedule."

"All right," Suzanne said. As she rose every male eye was upon her. She seemed to undulate to her feet, rather than simply stand and every ample curve of her body was in motion.

Brandon, from the corner of his eye, saw Cindy shake her head at this display, and couldn't keep a slow smile from forming on his lips. He saw, too, that Suzanne had taken notice of his smile, and was returning it with one of her own. *Watch out,* he cautioned himself.

He sensed someone walking beside him as he started toward the makeup area. He turned his head slightly and found that Suzanne had fallen into step next to him.

"Hi," she breathed. "Mind if I walk with you?"

Brandon shrugged, recalling her earlier words. "Were you really up for the part before Lorraine?"

"Yes, and boy was I mad when they cut me out."

"I bet you were, but I don't think Miss Rodman did what you said."

"She did. I can tell you *all* about it," Suzanne stated bluntly.

"Can you?" Brandon asked innocently.

"Try me," she whispered, her eyes open and inviting.

"Maybe I will," he said as he stared intently at her, his face wearing an expression that was all Suzanne had been hoping for.

"Any time," she breathed pointedly. "Any time at all." A moment later she veered off toward her waiting makeup girl.

She knows something, Brandon thought. But it wasn't what she'd been hinting at. Brandon knew he would have to be very, very careful in his dealings with Suzanne Roland.

"Over here, Mr. Michaels," called his own makeup man. Brandon tore his eyes away from the swiveling hips of the starlet and walked to the waiting stool. When the white cape was settled over his shoulders and the makeup man began to work, Brandon tried to clear his mind of what had happened, forcing himself into the character he was about to play.

"That one is something else, ain't she?" asked the makeup man.

"Which one?"

"Suzanne Roland. Some body, huh?"

"Is that so?" Brandon asked with a straight face. The makeup man paused to stare at Brandon for a moment before shrugging his shoulders and going on about his work.

Brandon and Elaine sat in the rear booth of a small country-and-western lounge, secure within its dark confines, relaxing for the first time that day. When Brandon had asked if she wanted to eat in tonight, Elaine had realized that she wanted to be as far away from the motel, and from the people involved in the film, as possible.

Brandon, after checking with the desk clerk about a decent place to have dinner, had picked her up and driven away from the motel. Twenty miles later they'd arrived at Dean's Place, as the neon sign proclaimed.

Brandon wasn't really a fan of C&W, but he liked it well enough, and had been told that of all the various night places one could go, a country lounge usually afforded the most privacy. The people who frequented these places were mostly hard-working, hard-playing individuals who respected a person's privacy.

And he'd heard right. Not once had they been disturbed, as they surely would have been back in town, where everyone knew about the movie. They were also protected by the fact that Brandon's face was not that well known outside New York's drama circles.

Elaine's thoughts were following a similar path. She was thinking about how lucky they were that Brandon was not yet as recognizable as some stars of his caliber, and that that would all change once the picture was released; because, after watching the rushes to date, she knew that no matter what fate the movie suffered, it would make Brandon a star, possibly a superstar.

But for now she was enjoying their relative anonymity, as well as the peaceful mood that encompassed them and temporarily helped to take her mind off the production troubles.

"How long will you be in Los Angeles?" he asked after the band finished playing a loud and plaintive song.

"I'm going to try to get back by night," she said.

"That would be nice."

"Brandon, I may lose the picture," she whispered, voicing the fear that had risen when she'd spoken with David Leaser earlier in the day.

"I doubt it," he said reassuringly.

"I don't. We're running behind schedule and we've got three and a half months of shooting left. I projected the cost figures again. If accidents keep happening, we'll be so far over budget that Cecil B. De Mille will look like a penny pincher."

"By today's standards, he was," Brandon joked as he reached across the table to cover her hand with his own. "Elaine, you're doing a good job, and I'm sure that Leaser will see the problems and troubles we're having have nothing to do with your abilities."

"Tell that to the stockholders," Elaine said realistically. "That's the bottom line, Brandon." Then she shook her head and smiled gently at him. "It's kind of funny.

We're both in the same business, working on the same project, yet we're so far apart in what we do. You have no idea of what it's like in the front office.''

"Why do you say that?" Brandon asked, surprised by this unexpected twist in their conversation.

"It's a lot like this movie, isn't it? I mean, the movie is a romance, and we're a romance. The movie is about people whose lives are far apart, yet close together. We're close, but what we do *is* far apart. We're in our own sort of distant world, so close but so different,'' Elaine replied in a faraway voice.

"Only if you think we are,'' Brandon said in a low, powerful tone. "The only distance in our world is in your mind. Try to remember that.''

She hesitated for a moment. "But that still doesn't solve the problem of tomorrow.''

"Why not wait and see? I doubt if Leaser will fire you.''

"I wish I was that sure.''

"I have enough confidence for both of us. Dance?" he asked. Without releasing her hand or waiting for an answer, he stood and led her onto the floor.

It was almost midnight when they left the lounge and drove the twenty miles back to the motel. Brandon had been very conscious of the problems that weighed on Lanie's thoughts, and when they went into her room and to bed, he kissed her lovingly; but instead of making love with her, he held her securely in his arms until she fell asleep.

When the alarm rang at four o'clock, Brandon woke her gently and they came together in a warm reaffirmation of their love, giving and taking from each other all they would need to make it through the day, until they could see each other once more.

Two hours later Brandon was on the set in his costume, having his makeup applied. Above him he heard the low whine of a private plane, and wondered if that was the one carrying Elaine to Los Angeles and her confrontation with David Leaser.

He was almost positive that she wouldn't get fired. He might not be in the front office, as Elaine had told him, but he knew the workings of the business end of a corporation well enough to know that Elaine's job was still secure. And, if necessary, he would exert a small amount of the power he possessed, a power few people knew about, that was on a level above even David Leaser's head.

"Don't you look pretty," Simon joked as he pulled up a chair next to Brandon's.

"That's what they pay me for."

"At least you can admit the truth." Simon fell silent for a moment, and when the makeup man had finished, he rose and motioned Brandon to follow him.

"Be careful!" admonished the makeup man, pointing to Brandon's face as the actor strode away.

When they were out of earshot, Simon stopped and faced his friend. "I made those calls yesterday."

"Good," Brandon said with a nod of his head. Before he'd left the set yesterday he'd called Simon over and asked him to make a few inquiries about Suzanne Roland. "And?"

"She'd never been considered for the part by Sellert. The casting director picked Lorraine herself."

"Was she consulted about Suzanne?"

"No," Simon replied quickly.

Brandon considered the information he'd just gained, and then made his decision. "I guess I'll have to take up that very open invitation of hers, won't I?"

"Brandon," Simon began, not liking the look that flashed across his friend's features, "you're playing with dynamite."

"Don't I know it. Simon, not a word to anyone. That includes your lady love!"

"Bran . . ."

"Don't give me that hangdog look. I've known you too long."

"All right, but I think it's a mistake."

"Places," came the amplified voice of the assistant director, effectively cutting off Simon's protests.

"I hope Elaine doesn't get wind of this."

"She won't be back until much later. Don't worry."

Then they were surrounded by the cameras and crew and their conversation couldn't continue.

"Brandon," John Hart called, "I want to do a walk-through with Suzanne first."

Brandon looked past Hart to where Suzanne stood, wearing a revealing costume. The starlet's most important possessions showed to their fullest advantage in a barely buttoned plaid top tucked into a pair of too-tight jeans.

Brandon smiled as the actress walked toward him. "I can't wait," he said. His tone was lost on her, but he did notice a strange, satisfied expression cross the director's face.

When work ended for the day, Brandon returned to the motel, where he found a message from Elaine waiting for him. In his room, with the door locked behind him, he called Trion Studios and was put directly through to her.

Ten minutes later, he'd hung up, reassured at the sound of her voice yet unhappy that she wouldn't be back until tomorrow night. Leaser hadn't fired her as she'd feared, but there were several things that needed her immediate attention in the office, and she had decided to spend the afternoon and tomorrow morning taking care of them.

That suited Brandon's plan perfectly; it would give him more time tonight to spend with a certain member of the cast. He hoped that by the time Lanie returned tomorrow he would have some interesting things to tell her.

Then his phone rang, and he answered it quickly. It was Chick Uldridge, and he wanted to speak with Brandon in person, and alone.

"Where are you?" Brandon asked, sensing something urgent in the man's voice.

"On location."

"I'll be there in twenty minutes."

What now? Brandon wondered.

Elaine signed the memo, put her pen down and leaned back in the chair. The day had gone very differently than she'd thought it would. She had expected a problem in dealing with David Leaser, but had been pleasantly surprised when her boss had seemed to understand the situation she was in on location.

After they'd watched the rushes and she'd given her progress report, Leaser brought up the subject of the shooting delays.

"It's not the first time a production has been plagued with petty thievery," he'd said.

"I think it's more than petty."

"Perhaps you should increase the guards," Leaser had suggested.

"I did. There are three men guarding the equipment and site," she explained.

"Hire two more."

"I don't think it's necessary."

"We have to keep it from happening again."

"I'm working on it," Elaine had told him. She also mentioned Chick Uldridge and what he was doing at night.

"It may help. Chick's a good man," Leaser had said.

"I hope so."

"How are you getting along with John Hart?" David had asked suddenly.

"With as little animosity as possible. He still resents me," she'd said honestly.

"Because of your father?"

"That, and because he thinks I finagled Sellert out and myself in."

"That's absurd."

"No, that's life."

"Elaine, perhaps it's time I had a talk with John . . ."

"No!" she'd snapped quickly, almost rising from the chair. "I'm the producer. I have to handle it myself!"

David had raised one eyebrow at her outburst. "For now, Lanie, but if there's more trouble, I'll have to step in."

"You mean replace me?" she had challenged defiantly, her anger gaining the upper hand.

"I hope not," he'd said ominously. "But if you need my help, I *will* expect you to call. Being a good producer also means knowing your own capabilities, and not being afraid to call for help. That's just as important as anything else, Lanie. Do you understand?"

She'd slowly nodded her head in acceptance of his words.

They'd talked for a half hour more about the various aspects of *Distant Worlds,* and when they were done it was lunch time. David took her to a small but often frequented restaurant where multitudes of movie people flocked each day. After an hour and a half of head nodding, hand shaking, and smiling, she'd returned to her office only to discover a mountain of paperwork that Bonnie had been unable to handle.

As soon as she'd seen what awaited her, Elaine had known it would be impossible to get back to Death Valley that night. She had called the motel, leaving a message for Brandon, and had begun to work.

Glancing at her watch, Elaine saw it was six-thirty. She rose and stretched, then walked to the door that separated her office from Bonnie's. Opening the door, she heard two voices outside, and realized that Bonnie hadn't gone home yet.

The women stopped talking when Elaine came out.

"I thought you would be long gone by now," Elaine said to her secretary.

"We were just leaving. Miss Rodman, have you met Joyce Seager?" Bonnie asked.

Elaine glanced at the woman and smiled as she prodded her memory. She recognized the woman, and knew she was a secretary, but couldn't recall whom she worked for. "Of course. How are you, Joyce?" she asked.

"Fine, Miss Rodman. How's the picture going?"

"Not bad, thank you. Bonnie, I'll be leaving in a few minutes . . ."

"Are you going back to the location?" Joyce asked

before Elaine could go on. "It must be very exciting for you."

"It is. But I'm afraid I won't be going back until tomorrow. Which reminds me, did you make the reservation?"

"All taken care of. The plane will be ready at two."

"Good. Oh, Bonnie, please take care of the things in my tray tomorrow morning."

"Consider it done."

"In that case, have a nice night," Elaine said.

The two secretaries left, and Elaine returned to her office, gathered her things and called for a company limousine to take her home.

The sun had set but the sky was still light when Brandon met Chick in the field office.

The stage manager had dark circles under his eyes, and Brandon realized just how tense and tired Chick was.

"I'm all ears," Brandon said the moment the RV door was closed.

"I'm not supposed to tell anyone about this, but I think I can trust you."

"You can," Brandon said.

"I spent last night in here, waiting to see if there would be another break-in."

"Why?" Brandon asked, surprised.

"After yesterday's film theft, I talked to Miss Rodman, and she was very upset. I thought that if I stayed here, maybe she would feel better. Besides, I don't think it's anyone from town."

"Oh?"

"Remember the fire?" Chick asked.

"How could I forget?"

"I think they're connected. Someone's out to sabotage the film."

"Why?" Brandon asked. He had his own suspicions about what was going on, but he wanted to hear Chick's.

"That's what I don't know. But I think that whoever is doing these things isn't doing it at night. It's happening during the day, and I think it's one of the cast or crew."

"How can you be so sure?"

"I watched the guards last night. They were on rounds all night long. When one took a break, the others changed their timing. No one is getting past them, Mr. Michaels, no one! Also, before I came to work for Trion, I was an MP in the army. I've seen a lot of break-ins. I'd bet anything that whoever is breaking into the equipment trailers has keys. I really think the damage to the locks is done after the break-in, because the tumblers were all unlocked when I examined them."

"If you're so sure, why are you speaking to me instead of the police?" Brandon asked.

"Because I've noticed something really strange."

Chick paused, and Brandon waited patiently for him to continue, his own thoughts racing a mile a minute.

"Since the trouble at the studio, we've had a closed set. Even here, no one is permitted in unless they have a pass or signed authorization."

"Yes?" Brandon prodded when Chick paused again.

"But they only check the people coming in. Not the ones going out."

Brandon stared at him as a glimmer of understanding began to surface in his mind.

"A few minutes before I called you I saw Hart leaving with someone. I don't know who it was, and when I asked a guard he didn't know either. But the one thing I did know was that everyone, except for Hart, myself, and the three guards, had signed out for the day. Hart should have left by himself.''

''It could have been one of the crew who had come back,'' Brandon said.

''Well, I did something else to check. That's why I decided to call you.''

''I have a bad feeling . . .'' Brandon whispered.

''I went into Hart's RV.''

''He left it open?''

''Studio property is my responsibility on location. I have keys for everything,'' Chick said with a conspiratorial smile.

''As it should be.''

''Mr. Michaels, someone's been living there. The bed's been used, and there's dirty laundry.''

''It could be Hart's.''

''I don't think so.''

Both men lapsed into silence for a few minutes, and then Brandon rose. ''All right, Chick, since you've decided to trust me, I've got a few things to tell you,'' Brandon said, and then he told Chick about his own suspicions, and the reasons behind them. When he had finished the stage manager was silent for a long moment.

''I'll keep my eyes open,'' Chick promised.

''I'll be counting on that,'' Brandon said as he left the office. On his way out, he noticed that the guards didn't stop him to ask for identification, but they did watch him until he started his car.

The phone rang only once before it was picked up. ''Yes?'' John Hart asked.

A moment later he hung up the phone, turned and smiled at the swarthy man sitting across from him.

"She's taking a two o'clock plane back. She should be at the location by three."

"Then you'll set it up for then?"

"I think that will work out just right. Especially after what happened tonight," John Hart said, his smile widening.

Filming had ended by three o'clock, and most of the cast and crew were gone. Brandon was sitting in the RV that had been assigned as his dressing room. He'd just taken off the day's makeup and, stripped to the waist, was relaxing with a glass of iced tea.

He was more tired than he should have been, but last night had been longer than he'd anticipated. When he'd returned from the location, he'd joined a group of actors who were sitting in the motel's lounge.

He'd chosen the seat next to Suzanne, and had appeared to be very interested in everything she'd said. An hour later they'd gone into the dining room together. They'd spent another few hours talking about their careers and about the movie, and Brandon had begun to ask leading questions about Suzanne's earlier remarks.

By the time dinner had ended Brandon was positive that Suzanne knew more than she was telling. But he'd also recognized the fact that she would do anything at all that enabled her to advance her career.

Throughout the meal, Brandon had been the recipient of an open invitation on Suzanne's face and in her voice, but he'd acted as if he didn't understand what she was offering.

After dinner, Brandon had walked her to her room. Outside her door she'd turned to him, her full lips glistening in the light of the hall.

"Would you like to come in for a nightcap?" she'd breathed in a throaty voice.

Brandon had smiled warmly, but had shaken his head slowly. "If I didn't have an early scene nothing could stop me," he replied as he bent lower.

She'd come up against him, pressing her overflowing breasts to his chest, her mouth open and hot against his.

Brandon drew back slowly, still shaking his head. "But I do have to get some sleep. I'll see you tomorrow," he added.

"That you will," she'd replied, her eyes narrowed, sultry.

That had been last night. And tonight Brandon knew he'd have to figure out some excuse to tell Lanie, so that he could continue to work on Suzanne.

A gentle tap on his door brought him back to the present and, rising, Brandon went to answer it.

Standing before him, a seductive smile on her lush mouth, was Suzanne Roland. "This is a surprise," Brandon said as he tried to gather his thoughts.

"I told you you would see me today," she stated, stepping inside and forcing Brandon back into the trailer.

"I meant tonight."

"I didn't want to wait," she said with another smokey look that left no doubt as to her meaning.

"Really?" he said with a smile as he moved in a half circle, following her movement. With his back to the door, he gazed down into her eyes. "Suzanne, I still would love to know what you meant yesterday about knowing how Rodman got Sellert dumped."

"Would you?" she murmured as she pressed herself against him. "How badly do you want to know?"

Taking a deep breath, Brandon realized it was now or never. He knew what he had to do, and slowly, he lowered his head and kissed her.

The kiss lasted too long, and Brandon was uncomfortable. He tried to draw his head back, but even as he did, Suzanne's fingers wound into his hair, and she pressed his mouth tighter to hers, her body continuing to move seductively.

"Oh, Brandon," she whispered against his mouth. Her voice seemed unusually loud in his ears, and it successfully masked the sound of the door opening behind him.

Elaine had parked her car in the almost-deserted parking area, and had walked past the guard at the entrance to the film site. She knew that the day's work had ended, but she hoped to catch Brandon before he left. She wanted to see him, to kiss him, to be held in his strong arms.

Halfway to Brandon's dressing room, she'd heard her name called and turned to see John Hart waving to her. Sighing at the inevitable, she waited for him to reach her, and because her back was turned to Brandon's trailer, she didn't see the young starlet walking quickly to it.

"Did you have a good trip?" Hart asked solicitously.

"Good enough. Any problems today?" she asked, against her better judgment.

"It was amazing; there wasn't a single problem. Perhaps you should go to Los Angeles more often," he suggested.

"Can't you give it a rest, Hart? Do we have to spend every day in a fight?"

"I really was joking," Hart protested, but Elaine knew better.

"Was there something in particular you wanted to talk to me about?"

"Yes. I've scheduled the helicopter scene for Friday. I also asked your assistant to requisition a backup copter in case of a problem."

"And?"

"He said to wait for you."

"I'll take care of it," she said, for once agreeing with the director.

"Thank you," he said. Then he simply turned and walked away from her. Elaine shrugged, then started toward Brandon's trailer, her heart racing with anticipation.

She was about to knock when she saw the door wasn't closed all the way. Smiling, she pushed it open and was about to step up when she froze. Her mind spun madly and she couldn't catch her breath. There stood Brandon, naked to the waist, and—Suzanne, she realized. Elaine was paralyzed, her legs refusing to move. Then she heard Suzanne's muffled voice crying out Brandon's name.

It was the starlet's voice that freed her legs, allowing her to flee the scene she had unwittingly witnessed. She thought she would be sick. Walking like someone in a dream, Elaine left the location and went to her car, unaware of the tears flowing down her cheeks. She didn't hear the sound of the car's engine when she revved it up—all she heard was the starlet's voice calling out Brandon's name. Again she saw him kissing her, and it hadn't been the light kiss of friendship so popular with theatrical people. It had been a deep, passionate kiss that had told her exactly what had happened in her absence.

Shaken to her very soul, Elaine drove straight to the motel, where she went into her room, locking the door behind her, and tried to erase the picture she had seen only minutes before.

How could he? she asked herself as the weight of his betrayal tunneled deeply into her heart. *How could I have been so stupid? Why did I let him have a second chance to hurt me?*

"Damn you Brandon Michaels!" she screamed with the full force of her lungs. Then, with her hands balled into tight fists, she sank slowly onto the bed.

Chapter 11

AN HOUR AFTER ELAINE HAD STUMBLED INTO HER MOTEL room, she was sitting in a chair, her mind still a mass of chaotic thoughts. She was in the grip of an anger fed by deception, lies and treachery. She hated herself for having been so gullible and hated Brandon for making her trust him.

But as the minutes passed she realized that she couldn't just sit there feeling sorry for herself. She had to do something. *But what?*

Rising, Elaine went into the bathroom, turned on the lights and stared at herself in the mirror. Her eyes were red-rimmed, but they hadn't become swollen. For that, at least, she was thankful. Turning on the faucet, Elaine rinsed her face with cool water.

''You should have known,'' she told her reflection. She could no longer deny the knowledge that Brandon was like all the rest of the people in his profession. Not like the superstars who had no need to use people, but like most of the ambitious film people who used anyone they could to advance themselves and further their careers.

Brandon had been using her for that purpose, she realized sadly. Why else would he want her? Elaine knew that many of the women in her business, especially the actresses, were beautiful—more so than she. How could she have hoped to compete with them? What could she offer Brandon that Suzanne could not? Intelligence? Did he want a woman with brains, ambition, the determination to follow through with whatever she started? "Apparently not," she told herself, again picturing Suzanne and Brandon in their heated embrace.

"Bastard," she muttered behind her clenched teeth. Then she knew that her own ego had been damaged badly enough to spur her on to teach Brandon Michaels a lesson. He might have fooled her but she wouldn't let anyone else be hurt by his callousness.

Pulling back her shoulders, shoring up her determination to assert herself, Elaine knew exactly what she was going to do.

After showering, Brandon dressed and left his room. He had been disappointed this afternoon when Lanie hadn't arrived at the location, but when he'd returned to the motel, he'd seen her car parked there. Instead of going directly to see her, he'd decided to take a shower first. He felt unclean somehow, contaminated by Suzanne's lingering scent. Sighing, he turned the corner toward Elaine's room.

It had taken all his patience to pry out the information

Suzanne supposedly possessed, which seemed to be very little. When he'd finally gotten rid of her, saving his virtue by pleading a backache and thus avoiding what she seemed to have in mind for them, he'd tried to figure out what part she was really playing in the entire scheme of things, but he hadn't been able to do so.

Suddenly a new thought struck him. It was only Elaine's fear of the others finding out about them that was allowing him to play up to Suzanne. If his relationship with Elaine were common knowledge . . . Perhaps that was a blessing in disguise, he thought. Brandon just wished he didn't get so angry when she insisted on it being that way. But he knew things would be different one day.

"Patience," he advised himself as he reached Lanie's room. He knocked on her door, and it opened a moment later.

He gazed at her, feeling the stirring of both his love and his desire. "Hi," he whispered as he bent to kiss her.

He felt her stiffen, and pulled back to look at her. "I forgot," he said in a level voice that didn't betray his inner turmoil at her behavior. He didn't speak again until he was inside with the door closed. "I doubt that anyone saw us," he said to reassure her.

"Brandon . . ." Elaine began when he finished speaking.

"No, I told you I understood. I didn't say I liked it, though. How was your trip?" he asked, trying to ease the tension that had flared up so quickly. "I gather you weren't fired."

"No, I wasn't," Elaine responded, searching his face and wondering how he could act so loving after what she had witnessed tonight. She forced herself not to think about that, to concentrate on her own little plan.

Then he was beside her, his lips covering hers, and despite the willpower she exerted, her heart began to pound and her blood turned hot in her veins. *No!* she commanded herself, fighting her body's reaction to his demanding kiss.

She fought harder as his kiss deepened, and almost lost the battle, but when he drew his lips from hers she regained a modicum of self-control.

"I missed you," he whispered against her forehead. The warmth of his breath across her skin sent a ripple of desire through her. Closing her eyes, she stopped herself from calling him a liar.

Then Brandon pulled back and smiled at her. "I'll call for dinner. We can relax and enjoy each other alone tonight," he said thoughtfully, knowing that Elaine would be more relaxed that way.

"No," she said suddenly. A slow smile formed on her lips before she spoke again. "Brandon, you're right. Our lives are our own, and we shouldn't let other people bother us. Let's go downstairs and enjoy ourselves openly." She saw at once the disbelief etched on his features.

Brandon's mind raced and the thoughts he'd had on the way to her room resurfaced in his mind. *Now what?* he asked himself. "Lanie, I think now would be the wrong time."

Elaine stepped away from him, unable to bear his deceitful touch. She stared openly at him, a challenge in her eyes. "Why? Isn't that what you want?"

"Yes," he said, "but right now would be—"

"Inconvenient?" Elaine hadn't meant to say it. She'd

wanted to force him into a corner, then make him face the music by going downstairs with her, but her anger removed the last restraints on her temper, and she lashed out at him. "Is that what you're trying to say?"

"Lanie," Brandon protested, taken aback by the anger and viciousness in her tone.

"Don't call me that! Only people I like call me by that name."

"What the hell is wrong with you?" Brandon demanded, surprised and puzzled at the same time.

"And don't you use that language either." Without giving him a chance to explain, she pressed on, rage lending force to her words. "Did you think I would just sit back and let you use me?"

"Use you? What are you talking about?"

"That's right, play the innocent. 'Oh Lanie, I love you. I need you.' Well, Mr. Michaels, you can play your games with someone else!"

Brandon's confusion gave way to his own anger. He didn't know what she was getting at, but he wouldn't stay still under her verbal onslaught.

"Lanie, make sense! You're acting like the rest of the idiots around here," he snapped.

"I told you not to call me Lanie! And if anyone fits into the description of an *idiot* around here, it happens to be you, Mr. Ego!"

Brandon reached out and grabbed her by the shoulders, imprisoning her. She fought to escape, but his grip tightened. "Stop it and listen to me!" he whispered in a harsh, demanding voice.

Elaine's eyes locked with his. "Why?" she asked. "So you can make me another pretty speech about your so-called love?"

"I want to know what you're talking about," he said in exasperation.

"Really? Let me go, then."

Brandon took a deep breath and released her shoulders. It was then that he noticed how moist her blue eyes were, and how close to tears she was. "Lanie," he began.

Elaine stared at him even as her hands went to her shoulders and massaged the spots where his fingers had dug so deeply. Her anger was dissolving, but not her hurt and anguish. There was still her love for him within her, and she knew that no matter how much she wanted to hurt him, to seek revenge, she couldn't do it.

"Brandon, I love you as I've never loved another person. When I look at you, especially when you're not aware of it, I want to scream out just how much I love you. All you have to do is touch me and I lose my self-control. I've given you my heart and my soul, and I've opened up and shared my most precious possession with you—my mind. Today I learned that I was nothing more than a fool—a twice-burned fool at that, who was being used by you."

Brandon heard her words, but still didn't understand what she meant. "Lanie, I don't know what happened today to make you think that, but I love you—"

"No, Brandon, no more lies," she pleaded.

"Lies!" The word exploded with the force of a bullet, and Elaine took an involuntary step backward. "I don't lie!" Brandon roared.

Elaine spoke calmly, in counterpoint to his shouting. "I arrived in Death Valley at three this afternoon. Fifteen minutes later I was at the location. I was so happy to be back, I almost ran from the parking lot to your trailer. I was about to call out your name, but I didn't. It was a good thing, too, because when I opened your door I saw just how much you missed me.''

Brandon shook his head slowly. ''You saw Suzanne and . . .''

''Yes, Brandon, I saw how much you love me.''

''I do, Elaine. What you saw wasn't real.''

Elaine's bitter laugh rang hollowly in the small room. ''Of course not, Brandon. What I saw was just an act, right? Are you going to tell me I made a mistake again, as I did in New York when I thought I was stopping you from killing yourself? Were you just getting into your role?''

''Lanie.'' Brandon hesitated after he spoke her name. He knew that no matter what he said, there was no way she would believe him.

''Don't you want to explain?'' she asked in the same calm, flat voice she had used before. ''Don't you want to tell me why what I saw wasn't *real?*''

''I could tell you that what you saw wasn't real, that I was doing it for you, but what's the point? You've already made up your mind. What bothers me the most is that in one breath you tell me how much you love me, and in the next you tell me how little you trust me. They go together, Lanie. You can't have love without trust.''

''What script did that come from?'' she asked, her words dripping acid.

''Your biography, I would imagine,'' he retorted sarcastically. ''No, don't say anymore, I can see in your eyes that nothing I say will be believed.''

''Why did you do it, Brandon?'' Elaine asked in a barely audible voice.

''For you, Lanie,'' he said. Then he turned, his anger at her lack of trust preventing him from saying anything more. With carefully measured strides, Brandon went to the door, opened it, stepped through and closed it gently behind him.

His mind was filled with turmoil, and he didn't want to go back to his room, nor did he want to see anyone else. Instead, Brandon went to his car, and a moment later he drove away from the motel.

Elaine stared at the closed door for an eternity. He was gone, and not in the way she had envisioned it would be. *Fool!* she called herself, remembering his empty words, the way he had tried to make her believe she'd been wrong about him and Suzanne. Did he think her a complete idiot? she wondered as she walked to the window. She saw Brandon's car pull out, and watched until it disappeared from sight.

"Good-bye," she whispered as she wiped away the tears that cascaded down her cheeks.

It was after midnight when Elaine returned to the motel. She'd spent the last few hours walking aimlessly beneath the star-filled desert sky, trying to clear her mind, to reassert her determination to survive the treachery of Brandon Michaels, and complete the film.

The unending pain that seemed to have become a part of her would not ease, and Elaine realized that nothing she could do would help—nothing would, except time. No matter what she was thinking of, Brandon's face floated before her. His touch burned along her body, and the many memories of their times together, times of loving and laughing, seemed to haunt her mercilessly.

Taking a deep breath of night air, Elaine returned to her room and the emptiness that awaited her there. But within moments she found she couldn't stand the quiet, and she reached for the phone. She felt a sense of relief when she heard Cindy's voice on the other end of the line.

"I need to talk to you," she said.

"Now?" Cindy asked in a sleepy voice.

"Please, Cindy."

"Give me a minute," Cindy said in response to the anxiety she had heard in Elaine's voice.

Two minutes later Cindy knocked on the door and Elaine let her in. She stared at her friend, unable to find a place to begin.

Cynthia, for her part, knew that something awful had happened the moment the door opened and she saw Elaine's tense face. Once they were inside, Cindy hesitated for a moment. Then she opened her arms, and her friend rushed into them and Elaine buried her head against Cindy's shoulder, finally able to give in to her tears.

Cindy held Elaine tightly, silently waiting for the first wave of emotion to pass. They had been close friends for so long that they could read each other's emotions well, and they knew, too, when it was time for words or for silence. Cindy realized this was one of those times when no words were necessary; her presence was enough.

Much later, when her sobs had diminished and her tears had eased, Elaine drew away from Cindy. "I'm sorry," she whispered as she wiped her eyes, "but I needed somebody."

"Don't apologize to me," Cindy admonished. "Are you ready to talk about it?"

Elaine shook her head. "I can't."

"Try."

"Cindy, I have to get it straight myself first. I thought I

had. God knows I've been walking for hours, thinking and thinking, but I just don't know what to do.''

''Is it the film, or Brandon?''

''Both, I guess. I know how much Hart hates me, and that he's trying to screw me up. . . . And I feel the pressure from everyone to get this picture right—not least of all, from myself. I want *Distant Worlds* to be good, better than good! But it's getting so damn hard.''

''And Brandon?'' Cindy persisted, hoping to get Elaine to open up the way she had that evening on the beach. She needed to talk, and Cindy hoped it would help her.

''Brandon is the movie's star. That's all he is.''

''What happened?''

''I'm not ready to talk about it, Cindy. I just needed a friend to be with right now.''

''And you have one. Lanie, whatever happened between the two of you, I know it will work out—''

''—for the best,'' Elaine finished.

''We've known each other too long,'' Cindy said lightly.

''Thank you for coming,'' Elaine whispered as she embraced her friend. When they parted after kissing each other good night, Cindy moved to the door.

''Cin,'' Elaine called, stopping Cindy before she could go. ''Don't say anything to Simon, please.''

Cindy nodded, then closed the door silently behind her. Elaine stood in the same spot for a few minutes before she could make her body obey her wishes. Moving lethargically, Elaine undressed and prepared herself for bed and, hopefully, sleep.

Simon rose through the foggy layers of sleep and realized the sound that had woken him was someone at his door. Getting up slowly, he reached for his robe. This wasn't going to be a good night at all.

After a lovely dinner, he and Cynthia had spent a few hours talking in the lounge before he escorted her to her room. He'd left her there to get a good night's sleep because she had an early scene to shoot.

He'd started for his room when he'd seen Brandon coming toward him. He'd stopped his friend, immediately seeing how upset the actor was. But when he asked him what was wrong, Brandon had shaken his head.

"Trust. Simon, she doesn't trust me. You know," Brandon had told him with a faraway look in his eyes, "she told me she loves me—not *loved* me. But she doesn't trust me!"

Simon had it figured out instantly. "Suzanne?"

"She found out."

"Tell her the truth," Simon had advised.

"Are you kidding? You can't speak to stone."

"Let me try."

Brandon had stiffened and glared at Simon with hard, piercing eyes. "If you value our friendship, you won't say a word."

Simon had held his friend's gaze, seeing that Brandon meant exactly what he'd said.

"Brandon, I'm sorry," he'd whispered.

"So am I."

The knock sounded again, and Simon moved faster. When he opened the door, he found Cindy waiting for him. "I thought you were . . ."

"I was, but I got a call."

"Are you okay?" Simon asked, concerned, as he stepped aside to let Cindy in. He closed the door and turned to look into her troubled face. "What?"

"It's Elaine and Brandon."

"You too, huh?" Simon replied. "We'd better sit down."

When they were seated in the swivel chairs near the room's single all purpose table, Cindy gazed at him. "How did you know?"

"After you went to bed I bumped into Brandon. He wasn't doing too well."

"Sounds like Elaine. But she wouldn't tell me what happened."

"Brandon was closemouthed too, but I did figure out that Elaine found out about his little episode with Suzanne."

"So?"

"I think she saw something she shouldn't have and got the wrong idea."

"Oh, no. But didn't he explain it to her?"

"He said something about talking to stone."

"That's Elaine. Well, now that I know what's going on, I can explain it to her."

"No!" Simon said loudly.

Cindy's head snapped up and her eyes widened.

"Sorry," Simon apologized quickly, and hurried on. "You weren't supposed to know about Suzanne. And Brandon asked me not to tell you about tonight, either."

"So?"

"We have to let them work it out themselves."

"But—"

"No. Brandon's friendship means a lot to me. I don't want to violate his trust. Please, Cynthia."

"Oh, Simon, they're like children; they love each other so much they can't see what's in front of them," she whispered. Then she moved out of her chair and into his

arms. "Don't let us get caught up in anything so silly,"
she pleaded.

"Never," he said, then he kissed her.

Elaine woke with a start, forcing away the last images
of the terrible, haunting dream that had held her in thrall.
She'd been dreaming that she was lost in the desert, far
from civilization, when she found herself at an oasis.

But she couldn't enter it because Suzanne Roland and
John Hart were standing guard. They laughed at her when
she tried to walk past them, then grabbed her and threw
her back out into the desert.

In the instant before she found herself facing the empty
expanse of sand, she'd seen Brandon sitting by a pond of
blue water, eyeing her helplessness with disdain.

Shivering, Elaine left the bed and went into the bathroom to wash away the dream and prepare herself to face
the day ahead. Twenty minutes later she was driving her
car toward the location, wondering just how she would
react when she saw Brandon.

When she arrived at the set she walked to the center of
the circled trailers and the long food table. She saw that
most of the cast had already eaten, and were now getting
ready for the first scene. Sighing with relief at not having
to face Brandon, Cindy or Suzanne, she accepted the cup
of coffee that Jason handed her.

"Bad news from Leaser?" her assistant inquired.

"No, just a bad night."

"Want me to bring you up-to-date?" Elaine nodded and
Jason told her what had happened in her absence, including Hart's request for another copter.

"Order the backup helicopter. The way things are
going, we just might need it," she told him. It was

pointless to add that Hart had already spoken to her. It was just another one of his ways of upsetting her staff needlessly.

"I also want to have a full cast-and-crew meeting tonight. I want to make sure everyone knows how important, and how dangerous, this scene is."

"Okay." Jason nodded.

"When is Hart scheduling the run-through?"

"Tomorrow afternoon."

"All right. Anything else?" she asked just as the loudspeakers came to life, calling for the first scene. Jason shook his head. "In that case, keep your eye on things. If you need me I'll be in the office."

Standing, Elaine looked around at the now scurrying people, but her eyes stopped when she saw Brandon coming out of his dressing room. Their eyes met and held for a long moment before Elaine, willing herself to be strong, turned away. Her heart pounded loudly and her stomach twisted, but she kept her face calm throughout the endlessly long walk to the safety of her office.

You can do it, she told herself, *you don't need him!* But when the door was closed behind her, she swore she could hear a faraway voice calling her a liar.

Brandon changed into his street clothes and stepped out of the dressing room. He joined the rest of the people heading toward the center of the equipment area and the commissary tables that were now being used for the staff meeting.

Throughout the day he had been aware of the fact that Elaine was avoiding him. But he had decided that this was not the time for a confrontation.

The day had been a strange one; throughout the filming

his senses had seemed to be blurred, as if his intuition was trying to tell him something—or warn him, he thought.

The director had been in a euphoric mood, so unlike his usual frame of mind that Brandon was puzzled. Hart's direction was light and smooth, without his usually overstated commands. That had only added to Brandon's concern.

When Brandon reached his seat almost everyone else was there. Elaine and Jason Heller were at the head of the table, and Hart was seated next to Elaine. As he gazed at them, he heard a whispered hello, and turned to see Suzanne sit down next to him, with a suggestive smile on her face.

When he turned back to look at Elaine, Brandon saw that her features had tightened. "Dammit all," he whispered.

"Are you speaking to me?" Suzanne asked, with her ever-present smile.

Before Brandon could say anything, Elaine rose and began to speak.

"First of all, let me say that the work you've done to date has been excellent. David Leaser has seen the rushes, and he asked me to extend his compliments. You can all take a bow." A round of applause greeted her words, and when it died down, she spoke again.

"This meeting won't last too long, which I'm sure you're grateful to hear." There was a small bubble of laughter and again Elaine waited for silence.

"The day after tomorrow we'll be filming the helicopter search scene. I just want to warn everyone that this will be a dangerous scene, and that you must follow both our director and the stunt director's instructions carefully. We can't afford any mistakes because loss of lives will be the penalty, not just delays. Now, I'd like to turn the meeting over to John," she said, favoring the director with a smile she didn't feel.

Hart rose and looked out at the seventy faces staring intently at him. "I'll make this sweet and simple. Tomorrow afternoon we do a full run-through. I want every cast member in the scene ready. There'll be three camera crews on the ground and one in the air. The ravine that we're working in is dangerous. Only the stuntmen are to go into it, is that understood?"

The nodding of heads signified everyone's acceptance of Hart's words. "In that case, I have nothing more to add, except that I want everyone to do the best they can. Remember, when I start the camera rolling Friday, I don't plan on making a second take." Hart sat down and Elaine rose again.

Elaine, in a rare moment, agreed with the director. She didn't want a second take either, considering that a second take would cost over a quarter of a million dollars. Helicopters, pilots and stuntmen were very, very expensive. But even the cost was a secondary consideration; there was always danger associated with film stunts, and having to do them twice doubled the risk.

"Unless anyone has anything to add, you're all free to enjoy the rest of the day. Crew, we expect you here by nine-thirty tomorrow. Cast, no later than eleven. The run-through is scheduled for one. Get some sleep," she concluded.

When the cast and crew had gone, Elaine found herself alone at the tables. She knew that she wouldn't be able to follow her own advice and enjoy herself tonight, but that didn't matter anymore. Only one thing mattered: that this picture be the best it possibly could. The thundering engines of a small fleet of helicopters, landing in the sand just outside the equipment area accentuated her thoughts.

"Are you sure no one will be hurt?" asked Hart, his voice betraying sudden nervousness.

"Relax, will you? I told you it'll be okay. The copter will be flying too low to sustain much damage. Everyone'll be shaken up, that's all."

"I hope you're right," Hart whispered.

"Hey, you getting cold feet? I thought you wanted her out?"

"I do," Hart protested. "I just wish Tom was here."

"We both know it would be too risky. Uldridge almost caught him the other night. No, it's better that he went back to L.A."

"This had better work," Hart said.

"Relax. After tomorrow she won't be bothering us anymore."

Chapter 12

ELAINE HAD SHOWERED AND DRESSED IN A CASUAL outfit of jeans and a loose-fitting top. She'd put on a pair of cowboy boots, and had brushed her hair away from her face. She didn't want to stay within the lonely confines of her room, and had decided to join the crew in the motel's lounge. That was something she hadn't done much of yet, mingling with the people she worked with each day. She hadn't because of her involvement with Brandon.

Besides, she realized, she had a reason to celebrate. There'd been no thefts, troubles or problems on the set in three days. *Maybe it's over with*, she thought hopefully. Before she reached the door the phone rang, and she veered toward it.

"Hello."

"Lanie, have you eaten yet?" Cindy asked.

"I was just going downstairs now."

"Join me?"

"I'd love to," she said truthfully.

"Great, I'll see you in a couple," Cindy said as she hung up.

Elaine smiled. Cindy was her lifesaver here. She didn't know how she would survive if it wasn't for her friend.

When she entered the crowded dining room, she was greeted by a dozen members of the film, who were all relaxing and enjoying the extra few hours they could have tonight because they could sleep in tomorrow morning.

The mood in the dining room was airy and the low hum of conversation was gentle against the background of piped-in music. The maitre d' came toward her just as she heard her name called, and she turned to see Cindy enter the room.

"Ready?" the actress inquired.

"Where's Simon?"

"Would you believe that ten minutes ago he came up with an idea he wanted to get down on paper? The first night in weeks we can stay up late and he ends up working," Cynthia said with a shake of her head. "The creative!"

"You should talk," Elaine retorted with a smile.

"Two?" asked the maitre d'.

Elaine nodded and he led them into the main section of the dining room, seating them at a small table by the wall. After taking their order of two glasses of white wine he placed the menus on the table and left.

"How are you?" Cindy asked the moment they were alone.

"Surviving," Elaine replied.

"That's important, too. Lanie . . ."

"Not now," she said, not even wanting to think of Brandon. "Ready for tomorrow?"

"Sure," Cynthia said in an offhand way.

"Did you go over the material with your double?"

"Yes, boss lady, I did. I've worked with her before, you know," Cindy said. "Relax, it'll go all right."

"I'm trying," Elaine said as she picked up the menu and glanced at it. "What are you having?"

"The chef salad looks good," she said just as their drinks arrived. The waiter served the drinks and then looked at the women expectantly.

"Two chef salads," Elaine ordered.

A moment later they were alone again. Cindy took a sip of her drink and stared at Elaine. "We have to talk about what happened," she said.

"No, we don't," Elaine retorted.

"Lanie, stop acting like a twit and listen to me!"

"'Twit'?" Elaine repeated as she stared harshly at her friend.

"Yes, you're acting like a spoiled little twit. I know what happened."

"No one knows, unless . . ."

"No, Brandon didn't say anything to Simon," Cindy said quickly. "Well, almost nothing. But when you saw Suzanne and Brandon, it . . . it really wasn't what it appeared to be."

Elaine sighed softly. "I love you, Cindy. You're my closest friend; you could be my sister. Please don't do this to me."

"I have to, Lanie," Cindy whispered.

"Then I have to leave," Elaine stated and started to rise.

Cynthia's hand shot out quickly, grasping Elaine's wrist in a tight hold. "Not till I say what I have to!" she said fiercely.

Elaine knew she could break Cindy's grip but she didn't want to fight. Shrugging, she relaxed her tightened muscles and settled back into the chair. "Go ahead," she said stiffly.

"Lanie, you're stubborn, strong-willed and sometimes a bit stupid and blind. Can't you see how much Brandon cares for you?"

Elaine did her best not to show the pain that Cindy's words caused her, keeping her voice on an unemotional level.

"I saw *just how much* yesterday in his dressing room."

"He was doing that for you!"

"I can't believe you're taking his side," Elaine whispered.

"Lanie, please try to understand what I'm doing. I'm risking my future by speaking to you about this."

"What?" Cindy's words had taken her aback and confused her once again.

"Simon explained what Brandon was trying to do with Suzanne, but he wasn't supposed to tell me. And I promised Simon I wouldn't tell you what I knew. If he finds out I'm breaking my word to him . . ." Cindy had seen Elaine's eyes flick away for a moment but she ignored it as she went on. "But I have to. Elaine, you love Brandon. The two of you are right together. And Brandon's only trying to help you."

Elaine had listened intently to Cindy but she'd seen something that had cut deeply into her heart.

"Cindy, I don't want you and Simon to have problems because of me. And I really don't want to hear how Brandon Michaels is trying to help me and that what I saw yesterday wasn't real. Not now!" she almost yelled as she rose and walked quickly away from the table.

Cindy turned to call out to her, but the words were trapped in her throat as her eyes fell on a table near them. It had been empty when they'd sat down but it wasn't any longer: Brandon and Suzanne were there now, holding hands and smiling meaningfully at each other.

"Dammit all," Cindy whispered angrily.

"Your table is ready," the maitre d' told Brandon, who smiled his thanks and called for his bar check, which he glanced at and signed. It was a pretty high tab, but he signed it gladly. Then he turned to Suzanne and offered her his arm. She took it, and Brandon observed the slight unsteadiness of her legs. *Good,* he thought.

For the past hour and a half he had been plying the starlet with drinks. Five, to be exact. He wanted her loosened up and ready to talk. Brandon fully intended to get some answers tonight.

They followed the maitre d' into the ornate dining room and to their table. Before he sat down Brandon glanced to the side and saw Elaine and Cindy. With a sinking sensation, he saw Elaine's blue eyes widen and then flick away from him.

Brandon sat down with a mental shrug, putting this latest incident from his mind and trying his best to concentrate on Suzanne. He would deal with Elaine when everything was settled.

"Cocktails?" asked the maitre d'.

"I think some champagne would be in order, don't you?" he asked Suzanne with a secretive grin.

"Oh, yes," she cooed.

"Perrier Joulet?" he asked the maitre d'.

"Excellent," he replied with a smile as he placed the menus on the table and left.

"Suzanne," Brandon began in a low, sincere, seductive voice. He reached across the table and took her hand in his. "Do you have any commitments after this film?"

He saw her eyes widen slightly, but then they changed into a calculating, penetrating gaze. "I have had a good offer," she said.

"I've liked working with you so far," he said as he squeezed her hand meaningfully. "I was hoping that we could do more together."

"So was I," she breathed, bending forward at the same time to show him a bit more of her cleavage.

"I have another movie after this one, and the lead female role hasn't been cast yet."

"Really?" she asked, suddenly returning the pressure of his hand.

Near him, a chair scraped against the floor, and a moment later he saw Elaine stride from the dining room. Once again he forced himself to forget her for the moment, to concentrate his attentions on Suzanne.

The waiter appeared then and, with great pomp and ceremony, opened and poured the champagne. As they lifted their glasses in a silent toast, he promised himself that he would get all his answers before the night was over.

———

The black expanse of the desert sky was broken by the pinpoints of 10,000 stars but it lacked the silvery sheen of the moon. It was a perfect night for the two men who were working quietly on the engine of the brightly painted helicopter. They worked steadily for a half hour, and then they left as stealthily as they had arrived.

In the field office, Chick Uldridge dozed lightly, his head resting on the Formica table. A wave of vertigo gripped him and he snapped his head up. Only then did he realize he had fallen asleep. Although he was angry at himself he knew he was paying the penalty for the last three nights of forced sleeplessness.

Getting to his feet, he looked out the window at the director's field office and thought he saw the quick flame of a lighter in the window, but it was gone too quickly for him to be certain. But the feeling that something was wrong was so strong that he threw away the caution and secrecy of the past nights and stepped out of the office.

He stood in the cool night air, allowing his senses to expand in an effort to discover what it was that was bothering him.

"You there! Freeze!" came the shout of one guard.

Chick did as he was ordered, and only when the guard's flashlight illuminated his face did he move.

"Sorry, Mr. Uldridge," said the guard quickly.

"Why? You were doing you're job."

"I know," the guard replied as he shifted on his feet. "But I'm a little jumpy tonight. Something in the air . . ."

"You feel it too?" Chick asked.

"Something's not right," the guard whispered.

"Let's look around," he said. Together, Chick and the guard began a close scrutiny of all the trailers and their locks. They were soon joined by the other two men.

When they reached Hart's trailer Chick turned to the guard who had spotted him. "Did Mr. Hart leave tonight?"

"About eight," he said.

"He came back at ten but left an hour later," said the second guard.

Chick stared at the trailer for a minute, his intuition

trying to tell him something. "Let's take a look," he suggested.

"Sorry, sir," said one of the guards. "Mr. Hart put a different lock on his door. He said he didn't trust the old one. He wouldn't give us keys, either."

"Really?" Chick said, more to himself than the others.

Brandon stood at the side of the bed, staring down at Suzanne without trying to hide the disgust that filled him. There was no need to, since the ripe-bodied starlet was sound asleep, dressed in a diaphanous negligee.

Brandon was still wearing the slacks and sports jacket he'd worn to dinner. He'd had no intention of taking them off at any point during their time together.

Stooping, Brandon maneuvered Suzanne under the covers, then turned away. She had passed out after changing into "something more comfretible" as she'd said, slurring her words.

When Suzanne had emerged from the bathroom, wearing the negligee and smelling as though she'd dumped a bottle of perfume over herself, she'd come over to Brandon and pressed her lush body against his. "We'll make a good team," she'd whispered seductively.

"But you said you already had an offer after this movie," Brandon had reminded her.

"I'd rather have an offer from you."

"Who's the picture with?" Brandon had persisted as he let his lips wander across her cheek.

"Ummmm . . . Sheller and Harsht," she replied, weaving her long fingernails through his hair.

Brandon couldn't figure that one out for a moment. Sheller and Harsht. Seller . . . Sellert and Hart, he'd realized suddenly.

"Hart hired you for the next picture?" he'd asked, drawing slightly away.

Suzanne had nodded lazily, then she'd shaken her head. "No, Sheller. Harsht's gwonna direck."

"They offered you the lead?" he'd persisted.

"Yup, and losh of money, too. They were shilly, weren't they?" She'd said, pulling out of his arms and twirling in a clumsy circle. She would have fallen but Brandon had moved quickly and caught her.

"See, you only think you caught me. I caught you. I told them I could," she'd said with a slow wink.

Everything began to fall into place then, as he deciphered the multiple meanings of her words. But before he could ask her another question she'd started to talk again.

"Do you really like me, Brandon?" she'd asked.

"Of course I do," he'd replied, pulling her close to emphasize his words.

"Good. Promish me you won't be mad if I tell you a shecret."

"I promise," Brandon said as his pulse began to accelerate and every nerve ending started to tingle.

"They promised me the lead part if I could sheduce you away from that uppity bish."

"Bish?" Brandon asked, startled at the unfamiliar name, wondering who Bish could be.

"Bish!" she repeated. Then she shook her head and tried again, enunciating very slowly, "Bitch," she finally got out."

"Oh," Brandon said.

"Yesh. Bishy Mish Rodman."

Then Brandon took a deep breath and smiled at her. "But you didn't have to seduce me away from anyone," he said pointedly.

"Don't tell that to them," she said with a wink. "They shink they got to her. Eshpeshially after yeshterday when she shaw us together."

"I see," Brandon said in a tight voice.

"You promised you wouldn't be mad."

"I'm not, I'm just starting to understand."

"Brandon, kish me," Suzanne whispered as she arched her back and parted her lips.

Brandon stared at her, willing himself not to be sick. Then, as he began to lower his mouth, he felt her body turn to rubber in his arms. She had passed out, he realized. That's when he'd placed her on the bed.

"Stupid," he told himself. It had all been for nothing. Although Suzanne had been a willing pawn in Hart and Sellert's game, she had known nothing. She was just a tool, and Brandon had fallen for the bait that had been offered, doing exactly what they'd expected him to do.

Suddenly Brandon wanted to talk to Elaine, to tell her everything that had happened, to try to figure out, with her help, a way to strike back and neutralize their enemies.

Brandon turned off the light, stepped out onto the walkway and headed toward Elaine's room, his face set in hard lines of determination.

Elaine had been unable to sleep, and had finally given up even lying in the bed; instead, she'd put on her robe and opened the curtains, and now sat staring out into the star-bejeweled sky.

She couldn't stop going over Cindy's words, which had been almost identical to Brandon's. She'd found herself listening suddenly, wanting to believe her friend and Brandon, but then she'd seen Brandon and that

. . . Brandon and Suzanne sitting at the table, holding hands, and she had known it would be hopeless.

She'd walked out of the dining room with her mind reeling under the twin assaults of rage and jealousy, and she'd realized that the jealousy was the worst of the two.

"Why couldn't you be different?" she asked Brandon's floating image. Then she shook her head to wipe away his image. "Sleep!" she commanded herself. But when she turned back to the bed she knew it would still be impossible to go to sleep and find the escape from reality she needed so badly.

A firm rapping at her door made her jump. She walked slowly to it and leaned against the wood. "Yes?" she asked, puzzled that someone would knock at this hour instead of calling.

"Lanie, open the door," Brandon said.

Elaine drew in a sharp breath and her heart raced at the aching familiarity of his voice. "I'm trying to sleep," she said in a voice just loud enough to be heard.

"If you don't open this door, I'll guarantee you won't sleep any more tonight!" he threatened.

A red curtain of rage flashed across her eyes at his words. Her hands moved quickly, unlocking the door and pulling it open. "Don't you ever threaten me!" she yelled.

Brandon stepped inside quickly, pushing Elaine back and closing the door in one smooth movement. Then he stared at her, a smile on his lips. "I thought that would do the trick."

"Did you?" she spat, growing even angrier at his confident words.

"I want to talk to you, explain about Suzanne. We were both tricked—"

"No more, damn you! I don't want any more lies. I won't listen to any more stories."

"Lanie, be reasonable."

Elaine forced herself to take a few calming breaths, and as she did so, she smelled the strong scent of a flowery perfume. Her eyes widened. "You hypocritical son of—"

"Bish," he finished for her.

Elaine was startled into silence by the strange word. "What?"

"It's part of the story. Let me tell it to you."

Elaine gazed into the depths of his green eyes and felt herself beginning to fall before their passionate call. Tightening her hands against her side, she took a step back.

"No, I won't let you fool me again. I can smell *her* all over you. You reek with her perfume. Did you at least wait for her to fall asleep before you came to me? Or were you both laughing at how naive I am? You—You—sad excuse for a thespian!"

Brandon's control slipped then, and his love for her combined with his anger at her refusal to listen pushed him over the threshold of his restraint.

Elaine's heart thudded loudly when she saw Brandon's features change dramatically. His jaw jutted out and his eyes turned to flint. She saw a muscle twitching in one cheek and suddenly knew she was in trouble.

In a flashing instant, he closed the space between them and caught her in his arms. He pulled her tightly to his chest, and even as she tried to turn her face from his, his mouth trapped hers and the burning brand of his lips was upon her.

She tried to fight her way free but the solid steel of his

arms held her to him. His mouth crushed hers, bruising in the intensity of his kiss. Then a fiery lance shot through her, and although she realized her body was betraying her again, she knew she couldn't fight it any longer—her love for him was too overwhelming.

Brandon felt Elaine fighting him, but didn't care. He would prove to her that he loved her! Then, as his kiss deepened and became more demanding, he felt her resistance begin to drain away. A moment later her lips softened, and he tasted the soft warmth of her mouth as it opened to him.

The kiss lasted for a long while, and when he finally loosened his arms and drew back his head, he knew he had broken down her stony defenses.

"Are you through fighting me? Are you ready to accept our love?" he asked.

Elaine gazed at him, aware of her misting eyes, and nodded slowly.

"Lanie, can we talk now?"

Elaine, knowing the true depth of her love and what she must do to protect herself, slowly shook her head. "No," she whispered.

Brandon stiffened and drew away from her.

"I love you, Brandon. If I hadn't known how much before this moment, I certainly do now. But," she said, stopping him from speaking, "I don't want to hear any more stories. I love you. Accept that and do whatever you want with me. Just don't tell me any more lies. And I . . . I won't ask you any embarrassing questions," she finished, her voice a broken whisper.

"What are you talking about?" he asked, genuinely puzzled by this latest turn of events.

"I don't want to know about you and . . ." She couldn't bring herself to say the other woman's name; instead, she turned her face from his.

"Look at me," he said in a low, icy tone.

Elaine kept her eyes averted, even as she stiffened at his command. An instant later his hand was on her chin, forcing her to look at him.

"Why do you refuse to listen to what must be said?"

"Because I don't want to hear any more lies," she whispered fiercely.

"I don't think so. I think you're afraid of yourself. You're afraid to trust me."

"How can I after—"

"After what?" he roared. "After refusing me the most simple of requests? After refusing to let me explain what you *think* you saw. I'm sorry, Elaine, but perhaps you should learn exactly what's involved in a commitment of love!"

"I should? What about you?"

"No more semantics, Lanie. I love you, but I won't stand here and beg. When you're ready to give me your trust, come to me. If not, well then . . ." Brandon let the last words remain unsaid as he stared at her. He hadn't meant for it to go this far, but he meant every word.

"Think about it, Lanie, think about it."

Before she could reply, Brandon turned and walked from the room, snapping the door closed behind him.

Elaine stared at the door with disbelieving eyes. Everything had happened too quickly, and her tumultuous emotions had yet to recover. Although barely a minute had passed since the door had closed, Elaine felt as if she'd been frozen forever in time. One word kept reverberating within the chambers of her mind—*trust*.

With trancelike movements, she forced her eyes from the door and walked to the window. "Trust," she echoed, wanting to be able to trust him but still afraid.

Then she looked down as a car roared to life, its headlights blazing in the night. Elaine froze, intuitively certain that it was Brandon.

She watched the car pull away, staring until the red taillights faded into the blackness that was the night, and her mind, as well.

"I love you," she whispered.

Chapter 13

ELAINE'S NERVES SCREAMED, AND HER SELF-CONTROL was on the thin edge of destruction as she watched all but one of the helicopters warming up. The combined thunder of the three helicopters was enough to make everyone shout in order to be heard.

Almost all of the cast and crew had left for the shooting location twenty minutes earlier. Now the pilots, the two cameramen, and the stuntman double for Brandon were about to go.

Something was bothering Elaine as she stared at the helicopters. That it had to do with Hart's strange change of plans, she already knew, but there was more to this feeling. Cindy's note hadn't helped either.

She had arrived at the equipment location at nine, after spending what remained of the night deep in introspection, which had done nothing to settle her troubled mind.

But when she'd arrived, she had been greeted by Hart, who said that he was altering today's run-through. It would still be a run-through but he wanted to film it.

While she had been talking with the director she had seen Suzanne Roland walk unsteadily into the area, on her way to the hairdresser's trailer. Her straw-colored blond hair was disheveled, her skin pale and ashen, and the dark circles under her eyes spoke clearly of her poor condition.

Doing her best to ignore the surge of jealous anger that had welled within her, Elaine turned back to John Hart's insidiously grinning face to ask a few more questions about the changes he wanted.

Although Elaine had not said so right away, she had seen the wisdom of filming the scene as a rough, in order to hone tomorrow's shoot to perfection. The only additional costs would be in the film and processing.

Agreeing reluctantly without understanding why she was so hesitant, Elaine had gone on to her office. As she walked to the RV, she'd seen Brandon emerge from his dressing room, wearing the same clothes he'd been in last night.

Her heart tugged at the sight of his handsome face and his disheveled clothing and she realized he'd spent the night here, but she knew this was not the time or the place for them to have another of their loud confrontations.

Once again denying the needs that assailed her, Elaine had gone into her office, where she'd waited alone until Jason Heller had informed her of the cast and crew's imminent departure.

"I'll drive out after the copters have left," she told him. "You go ahead and keep an eye on everything."

Jason had smiled and winked. "I've got everything covered," he'd said confidently as he'd waved good-bye to her.

When he'd gone Elaine had sat back in her chair and thought about Jason. He'd been a good assistant, taking on much more responsibility than required. He had helped her a good deal, Elaine realized, and made a mental note to not only thank him, but to ask for him on her next picture. "If I get a next one," she'd whispered.

Then her door had opened again, and Cindy was staring at her. "This is for you," she'd said, dropping a sealed envelope on the table. "Read it if you value our friendship." Before Elaine could say a word, Cindy had turned and walked out, slamming the door behind her.

Hesitantly, confused by Cindy's cryptic remark, Elaine picked up the envelope, opened it and withdrew a single piece of note paper.

She read it carefully, then reread it. When she was done she closed her eyes and forced herself to hold back her tears. The note was short and to the point—Brandon had been trying to gain information from Suzanne about the troubles on the set. Cindy had risked her relationship with Simon to tell Elaine the truth. Elaine promised herself that Simon and Brandon wouldn't learn of it. But now she found she could understand everything that had happened, and she realized that Brandon had told her the truth.

Elaine vowed that later, after the run-through, she would apologize to Brandon for her behavior, and then let him explain what had happened with Suzanne, without telling him she already knew. Then she'd left her office and gone to make sure the helicopters took off without a hitch.

Watching the three ungainly metal birds as they began

to build up power, she found herself wishing that she was at the controls of one. It had been over a year since she'd flown the ranch's copter, and she suddenly missed the scary and exciting feeling that was so much a part of flying a helicopter.

Then the whirlybirds were in the air, and Elaine, with her hand shielding her eyes from the glare of the sun, watched them zoom upward. When she lowered her eyes she saw the large form of Chick Uldridge walking through the area that the copters had just left.

She saw him studying the ground carefully as he walked, and watched him stop to look at something there. Shrugging her shoulders, Elaine reached into her pocket and withdrew the car keys. She would arrive at the filming location just after everything started.

Turning, Elaine began to walk toward the parking lot, but Chick's loud shout stopped her. Spinning, she saw the stage manager waving his arms frantically.

With a shiver of intuition coursing along her spine, Elaine ran to the stage manager.

"What?" Elaine called when she was closer to him.

"I don't know. I felt that something was wrong all night, so after the helicopters took off I came over to look around. Everything seemed all right, but then I found this," he said as he pointed to a small dark stain on the rocky ground.

Rather than shrug off Chick's concern, Elaine bent and looked closer at the small, oily patch. "Was anybody working on the copter?"

"Not yesterday afternoon, and not today. I was watching them," Chick stated emphatically.

As Chick spoke Elaine ran her index finger across the puddle. Whatever it was, it was too thick to be absorbed by the sand and rocky ground. Lifting her finger to her nose, she sniffed.

She smelled a faint tar base to the oily stuff, but that only added to her confusion. Then, as she stared at her now brown-stained finger, another chill raced along her spine as her memory was jogged by something she'd seen earlier.

Elaine thought back to her summers on the ranch and the lessons she'd learned about helicopters. Although the ones they were using in the film were not the same as the one at the ranch, they were turbine-powered. And the most important thing to remember about a turbine engine was to make sure the fuel was uncontaminated. A contaminant could clog the fuel line, cutting off the gas to the engine, and that would be disastrous.

"Which copter was this under?" she asked in a tight voice.

"The one in the film," Chick stated.

Elaine's heart lurched when she realized that it was the copter that was carrying Brandon and his stunt double. "Oh, no," she whispered. She turned toward the car and then stopped. "Not fast enough!" she shouted to herself. Turning back again, she stared at the fourth copter, the one that Hart had ordered—just in case.

Just in case, nothing! Elaine knew then, with all the intuition she possessed, that something would happen to the copter that Brandon was in.

"Chick, let's go," she said as she began to run across the ground in a straight line toward the helicopter. Once she was seated, and had made sure Chick was strapped in, she started the engine, waiting impatiently until it had warmed up enough.

"Miss Rodman?" Chick asked, watching her hands perform a dozen different chores on the instrument panel.

"I'll explain in a minute," she told him as her feet went to the pedals and her hand pulled back on the stick.

Chick swallowed hard as she took the copter up into the air, and said a silent prayer that she knew what she was doing.

But Elaine took no notice as the memory of a grease-stained hand, (one that that had no reason to be in that condition,) flashed into her mind's eye. *Why?* she asked herself.

Brandon stared across the expanse of whitish rock and desert sand, observing the somewhat vegetated hills at their sides and the denser, more barren stretches of Death Valley far ahead of them. He tried to get his mind back onto the matter at hand, but last night's confrontation with Elaine was still troubling him.

After leaving the motel he'd driven to the equipment location, signed in with the guards, and walked to his RV. Before he'd had a chance to open the door Chick Uldridge was at his side, wanting to speak with him.

A half hour later, Brandon and Chick were walking around the complex with one of the guards, checking everything over again.

When he'd finally returned to his RV, after saying good night to Chick and telling him to get some badly needed sleep, he found it impossible to follow his own advice.

His frustration increased at not being able to get through to Elaine. Not even Chick's sudden and obsessive worry that something had been tampered with was enough to take his mind from Elaine.

He'd sat up all night, and when the sun had risen he'd made some coffee, again lost in thought.

He'd finally forced himself to leave the dressing room around nine, and he'd stepped into the brilliant sunlight to find Elaine staring at him from across the way. His need and desire had surged upward like shooting stars, but he'd stayed where he was, and Elaine had turned and disappeared into her office.

Shaking his head, Brandon had gone for a walk.

"Comfortable?" asked the helicopter pilot. His voice crackled with electricity in Brandon's helmet.

"Fine," Brandon replied.

A shudder rippled through the cockpit and Brandon turned to the pilot. "What?"

"Nothing, probably just an impurity in the fuel," he said in a relaxed tone as his fingers manipulated the controls. "Don't worry about a thing."

"I won't," Brandon said with a smile. Then he felt a finger tapping him on the shoulder and turned to look at the stuntman.

"Let's talk it through," the stuntman said. Brandon nodded and the man went on. "We're doing this as if it was the real take. The film copters will be ahead of us and on the side. They'll take close-ups of you looking out and putting on the harness. Then you'll lean out."

Brandon arched his eyebrows.

The stuntman laughed and patted him on the shoulder. "Don't worry, I'll be holding on to your harness. After you get back in, we'll switch seats. We have to do it smoothly because they'll be shooting the outside of the copter," he cautioned. Again Brandon nodded in understanding.

"After we switch you stay low behind the seat. I'll go

down and rescue the girl. After the footage is shot, we'll go to a level spot and do a few close-ups of you in the harness, suspended from the copter.''

"Wouldn't it be easier if I just did the rescue myself?'' Brandon asked, only half-joking.

"What? and me lose my chance at stardom?'' asked the stuntman, returning Brandon's grin.

Even if Brandon had really wanted to do the scene, the studio wouldn't have permitted it. He might have to be in the copter, but that's as far as it would go. No unnecessary chances were taken with movie stars—hospital stays weren't figured into the budget.

"Here we come,'' said the pilot.

Brandon and the stuntman both looked out and down. Below them was the deep, narrow ravine that was the spot for the shoot. A quarter of a mile away were the vehicles that had brought everyone out, and lining the side of the desert cleft was the cast and crew, all set up in their film spots.

"Ready?'' came the voice of John Hart over the radio.

"Ready one.''

"Ready two.''

And then Brandon's pilot spoke. "Ready three,'' he said as he maneuvered the copter over the ravine and held it motionless in the air.

"All right, boys,'' came the voice of the stunt director, Wally Mason, who was in the copter directly in front of Brandon's. "Let's do it on the down count. And, three, two, one!''

Brandon moved into action, wriggling into the harness, keeping his body facing forward so that the camera in the copter in front could take the necessary shots.

"Nice, very nice,'' said the stunt director when Brandon was finished. "Okay, Brandon, nice and slow, slide the door open and start leaning out. Mickey, don't lose him. We have to get another close-up first," Wally joked.

Brandon leaned a full third of his body out, and was surprised at the intensity of the air hammering at him from the copter's blades. He stayed in position and began to scan the ground below. Although he was conscious of the two other helicopters, especially the one low and on the side, he trained his eyes on the ground. Then he saw Cindy and her double in a tangle of rocks within the ravine.

"Good, now wave to her," said the director.

Brandon took a deep breath, released his hold on the side of the copter and waved to the actress below.

"Back in," said the stunt director and, as Brandon started back in, he felt Mickey pulling on his harness. "Okay, Brandon, that was nice. Now switch with Mickey —fast."

Without conscious thought, Brandon squeezed himself into the back of the copter as Mickey moved up front. A second later, the switch was complete.

"Mickey, hook up on the line."

Brandon, bending low so he would be out of camera-range, watched the reflection of the stuntman in the glass on the side of the copter. Suddenly another shudder rocked the cabin, but it passed almost instantly.

"What the hell was that?" Mickey asked.

"What?" came the voice of the stunt director.

"Nothing," said the pilot, who was again adjusting one of the controls.

"You okay?" asked the director.

"Fine. It may be a bad load of fuel. It seems okay now."

"Want to break off?" asked the director.

The pilot rechecked his gauges carefully before replying. "Everything's running smoothly now . . . it looks okay."

"All right, let's get going," the director said. "Mickey, nice and easy."

Brandon waited until the stuntman was out of the copter before he moved. Slowly, he leaned over the seat and stared at the descending man as the director's voice continued to exhort the cameramen in the other copters.

"How's he doing?" the pilot asked, his face carved with lines of concentration as he stared at the panel of gauges before him.

Glancing down again, Brandon saw that the stuntman was almost on the ground. Before he could answer the pilot the director's voice cut in.

"Down a little, Bill," the stunt director ordered. "Move it around, make like you're in a heavy wind."

Brandon watched the pilot begin to do his thing and heard the copter's engine whine as he maneuvered it about to create the effect needed for the scene.

"Good, good, Mickey's swinging like he's Tarzan. Very nice. Okay, Bill, shoot up twenty feet and then drop back, just the way we planned."

The pilot gave the engine more thrust, and the copter spun about and started upward. Just as it reached the peak the engine began to cut out.

"Trouble!" shouted the pilot while he fought the controls and did his best to keep the helicopter level.

Brandon felt a charge of adrenaline burst into his bloodstream as he sat helplessly by.

"Mickey," the pilot shouted in a tight voice, "winch up. Quick, I can't hold it much longer."

Brandon spun in the seat and hung half out of the copter, trying to see if Mickey was all right. The copter was moving erratically, and he saw Mickey graze the side of the ravine and bounce wildly about. Then the stuntman began to rise slowly.

"He's coming," Brandon said.

"Hurry," he heard the pilot whisper, the tension in his voice amplified by the helmet.

"Bill, can you hold on?" asked the director, his voice flat and strangely calm.

"I'll have to," he said.

Brandon braced himself as another series of engine misses shook the copter. His stomach lurched as the copter plummeted sharply near the edge of the ravine. There was a sudden tug at the bottom of the copter and Bill fought madly to regain control of the faltering machine. Brandon realized that the cable had hit the side of the ravine. *Mickey!* his mind screamed as he wondered if the stuntman had survived the collision.

"Dammit, Mickey, where are you?" yelled the pilot, echoing Brandon's unspoken thoughts.

Forcing himself to move, Brandon leaned further out and saw that Mickey was spinning at the end of the cable. The winch was not pulling him up.

"Something's wrong," Brandon shouted. "The winch isn't working."

The pilot's hand went to yet another toggle switch, which he flipped several times. "The line is jammed. It must have happened when it hit the side of the ravine," the pilot said in an almost matter-of-fact voice.

Then the stunt director cut in quickly. "Bill, you've got to get out of the ravine. Get some altitude and then set him down on the other side."

Brandon sat up and looked at the pilot. He knew the answer before the man spoke.

Brandon started talking before Bill could say anything. "Let me go out. I can try to pull him up by hand."

"I can't," the pilot replied.

"What else can we do?"

The pilot looked at him for a moment but didn't speak.

"Brandon, no!" screamed the stunt director.

Ignoring the man's order, Brandon slid out of his seat and grasped the side of the copter tightly. Carefully, aware of every movement he made, he drew his body out and, secured only by his hands, searched with his feet until he found the struts.

Once his feet were set, he slowly squatted, holding on to the metal struts until he was in a position to maneuver himself. The first thing he did was to examine the cable. At the junction where the thick metal wire disappeared into the copter, he saw several torn and jagged pieces that were obviously preventing it from working.

Then he hooked his harness's safety rope around a strut and clipped it into place. Carefully, thankful that he had been told to wear the same kind of gloves the stuntman had on, he grasped the steel cable in his hands and began to pull up on it.

A moment later he was rocked about, and the cable slipped out of his hands as the copter lost more altitude.

Once again, Brandon set himself for the task, willing his muscles to hold out.

It took Elaine a few minutes to get used to the idiosyncrasies of this particular helicopter, but she did that while she navigated the copter at its greatest speed toward the deep ravine that was being used for the filming.

After they were on their way, she glanced at Chick and saw the tense expression on his face. She pointed to the helmet on the floor and motioned for him to put it on, and she donned one as well. Then she opened the com-link between them.

"Relax, I know how to fly this thing," she said.

"I kinda figured that one out," he said in a low voice.

"All right. I hope I'm wrong, but I think someone tampered with the copter's engine. I think they fouled the fuel."

"Why?" Chick asked.

"To sabotage the movie."

"Miss Rodman, they're only doing a run-through. Even if something happened to the copter, we have this one for the real shoot."

Elaine had already realized that, and had also foreseen the consequences. This was not just a little stunt to hold up production. This was the kind of sabotage that could destroy the movie and conceivably kill the movie's star, not to mention spelling the finish of her own career.

But none of that concerned her. All that mattered was that she get there in time or that she be wrong, that everything she had dreaded be only a bad dream, a mistaken conclusion.

The copter burst across a rise, and Elaine caught her breath when she saw the three helicopters in the distance. She adjusted the radio receiver until she heard the voices coming from them, and then her heart checked and threatened to stop beating.

She saw the stuntman hanging beneath the bouncing copter, and heard the stunt director yelling at Brandon not to go out.

She shoved the throttle forward, and the copter responded instantly to Elaine's touch. "What's going on?" she demanded over the radio as she watched Brandon secure himself to the landing struts and reach for the winch's cable.

"The engine's fouled, winch jammed," the director stated bluntly.

Elaine reassessed the situation, and then spoke directly to the pilot of the crippled helicopter. "Can you climb ten feet higher and get out of the ravine?" she asked as she swooped her copter lower and entered the ravine.

"I don't know. I may blow the engine entirely."

"Try," she pleaded in desperation.

"Just who are you, lady?" asked the stunt director.

"Rodman, your boss," she snapped. "Now stay out of this unless you can do something with those other copters."

"I wish I could," he whispered into the microphone.

Elaine swallowed nervously. Suddenly she was remembering the first time she had met Brandon, on the Brooklyn Bridge. She could hear his voice telling her about the old Chinese custom—that she was responsible for his life once she had saved it. *I will be, if I can,* she vowed to herself.

"Brandon, can you hear me?" she asked, fearing what she knew had to be done next. If they were lucky, the sabotaged copter would have a few more minutes of air time, barely enough for her to do what was necessary.

Brandon could hear her. He had recovered from his initial surprise at hearing her voice and was concentrating his attention on the cable. As he pulled up on it, he grunted in reply.

"The pilot is going to try and get Mickey over level land. What we have to do is tricky. Look at the cable. Is it torn at the base of the winch?"

Brandon, his arms screaming in protest at the weight he was holding, didn't bother to glance at what he'd already seen. "Yes."

"Bill, try the winch, but lower it."

A second later, the cable moved down freely.

"It's moving!" Brandon cried.

"Hold it!" Elaine ordered. "Brandon, let the cable go free," she said. She watched two things happen at once. Brandon released the cable, and the pilot urged the copter up another few feet, clearing Bill from the ravine and moving over above level ground.

"Brandon, the next part is the hardest. First clip your safety harness to the cable. Then slide down to Mickey. Brandon, it's our only chance," she added.

What she didn't add was that it was one chance in a million. "Bill, when I tell you, lower the cable all the way."

"What the hell are you going to do?" asked the stunt director.

"Save their lives," Elaine whispered. "Brandon, when you reach Mickey, grab on to him. I'm . . . I'm going to try to get a little lower than your copter's blades. We're going to have to try a circus act. I'll come in low, and as close as possible. Chick's with me. He's going to be out on the struts, too. He'll swing our cable to you. You'll only have one chance. Grab it, hook yourself to it, and then release Mickey's safety, hang on to him and pray."

"Thanks, boss," Brandon said dryly as he reached the unconscious form of the stuntman.

"Brandon, trust me," she whispered.

"I always have," he replied.

"Chick?" she asked as she lowered the copter and pressed the winch release at the same time.

"On one condition."

"What?" Elaine almost screamed.

"When we find out who did this, he's mine."

"I already know," she told him. Chick sat still for a moment, and then he began to move. "Be careful," she told him.

The big stage manager slid the copter's door back. Then he was outside. He fought the buffeting winds and, gloveless, began to swing the winch's cable back and forth while Elaine maneuvered the copter as close to Brandon as possible.

"Hold it, Bill," she said to the other pilot.

"I'm losing it," he responded.

Elaine was frantic, her heart beating like a trip-hammer and sweat pouring down her face. She tilted the copter slightly, hoping that Chick could hang on and get closer to Brandon and Mickey.

"Almost," Brandon called, and Elaine heard the desperation in his voice. "One more pass."

"Dammit, Brandon, if you love me, do it now!" she screamed, her senses telling her that it was now or never.

"Got it! Hold it, Lanie!" Brandon cried. Frantically, he grabbed the second cable with his free hand and brought it to his waist. But he had no intention of hooking himself up first.

Moving with every bit of strength he possessed, he hooked Mickey's secondary safety line to the cable from Elaine's helicopter. Only then did he secure his own line to the new cable. With his muscles screaming in protest, and as he fought the backwash of air from both helicopters, Brandon released the cable catch on Mickey's harness. The instant the stuntman was freed, Brandon unhooked himself and swung away from the damaged cable.

In Brandon's perception time had slowed, and everything seemed to take forever, but to the observers below and in the other two copters, Brandon had moved with the speed of lightning. The transfer had taken less than forty-five dangerous seconds.

The sudden pull of extra weight told Elaine that she had won. Sighing, she pushed the controls sideways and, as she pulled away from the other copter, she leveled her own.

"Take her down, Bill," she said.

Bill breathed his own sigh of relief, and started straight down. When he was ten feet from the ground, the engine gave one last rumbling revolution and shut down. But he had been low enough, and he was able to manage a fairly soft landing. But it was nonetheless a landing that would have killed anyone hanging beneath the copter.

Elaine shuddered when the copter fell the final ten feet and choked back the bile rising to her throat when she saw the landing struts crumple under the weight of the fall.

"Brandon," she called in a husky voice.

"Here, Lanie," came his amplified reply.

"I'm going to set you down slowly. When your feet are on the ground, let me know. I'll hover until you get yourself and Mickey clear."

"Lanie . . . thank you," Brandon said softly.

Rather than reply, Elaine called to Chick. "Can you make it back inside?" she asked.

"I sure as hell ain't standing out here when you land,"

the stage manager replied. A moment later he dragged himself back into the cockpit.

"I don't think I've ever done anything that scary before," he told her.

"Me either," she said truthfully.

Then she slowly and carefully lowered the copter, making sure that her every movement was precise. She was concentrating so intensely that she failed to realize that no other voice had spoken since she'd started the rescue operation.

"Hold," came Brandon's voice in her helmet. "Mickey's down. I'm down," he added quickly. Elaine breathed another sigh of relief as she raised the copter. She pressed the switch for the winch, and when it was secured within its case, she lowered the helicopter and landed it with hardly a jar.

She stayed in her seat for a moment and then reached for the ignition switch. Just before she touched it, a voice rang in her ears.

"Miss Rodman . . ." called the stunt director.

"Yes?"

"Thank you, that was a hell of a job," he said simply.

Chapter 14

ELAINE TOOK OFF HER HELMET AND TURNED TO look at the other helicopter. She saw the pilot standing next to it, looking at it strangely. Then she turned and saw Brandon walking toward her.

Her breath caught in her throat and her eyes misted. She'd almost lost him again, this time to an enemy she couldn't fight.

"Miss Rodman," Chick called from behind her. Elaine turned and looked at the ashen-faced stage manager.

"Are you okay?" she asked.

"I will be. Who was it?" he asked.

"Not yet. Come with me," she told him as she unbuckled her safety belt and hoisted herself out of the copter.

She saw everyone running toward them as the other copters landed. She watched Hart get out of one copter and try to hang back, but he was dragged along by the others.

Then Brandon was there, and she was engulfed within his arms. His lips met hers in a gentle yet fierce kiss that said everything in the world to her.

"I love you," she told him.

"I know."

She stared into his eyes, searching them, and then across every inch of his face. "Bran . . . I've been a fool. I . . ."

"Trust you," he whispered, finishing her words for her.

"I was wrong—about a lot of things, including Suzanne and you. I acted like a fool; I see that now. I'm just sorry I had to learn this way."

"But you did. That's what counts. Now, I have something to do," he told her, his voice changing to a tone that barely contained his overwhelming rage.

Elaine followed his eyes as they searched the crowd. Then he released her and walked slowly toward Hart.

The director saw the rage etched on Brandon's face and started backing away. "Hold him!" Brandon shouted, pointing at the director.

The cast and crew stared disbelievingly at Brandon's pointing finger, but the stunt director, who was standing next to Hart, turned and grasped him tightly.

Elaine froze when Brandon started forward because, from the corner of her eye, she saw another man turn and begin to edge away from the crowd.

"Chick," Elaine whispered fiercely, "get him." She pointed to the retreating back.

Chick started off at a run, and Elaine, knowing that he would catch him, followed Brandon.

Brandon walked purposefully toward Hart, anger making his steps stiff and jerky, and when he reached him, he drew his arm back, his large hand curled into a fist.

"You bastard," Brandon hissed as he started to swing at the man. But he stopped himself and just stared into the terrified, small, gray eyes of the man who had almost killed him.

"Where's Sellert?" he asked.

"Sellert?" Hart replied, startled by the question.

"Don't play stupid with me. I know you and Sellert were behind everything that's happened here. Suzanne told me all about it," Brandon said.

"You're crazy!" Hart snapped. "You're a madman!" Then Hart turned to the stunt director. "Let me go," he ordered.

Brandon saw the indecision in the other man's face and shook his head. "Hold him."

"You won't get out of this one, Hart," Elaine said as she stepped between Brandon and the director. Her own anger was strong, made even stronger by Brandon's accusation against Tom Sellert, whom she hadn't connected with what was going on; but what Brandon had said made sense.

Then she saw Hart's eyes widen in fear and turned to see Chick Uldridge manhandling a tall, slim man.

"I'll be da . . ." Brandon began, as Elaine slipped her hand into his.

"Was it him, Miss Rodman?" Chick asked.

"Was it you, Jason?" she asked, staring into her assistant's dark eyes.

The assistant director didn't say a word. He only glared at her.

"Why, Jason? Why, Hart?" she asked, whirling about to confront the director again.

"You're crazy!" Jason Heller shouted.

Brandon stared at him, and then at Elaine. Suddenly he remembered last night and the drunken words of Suzanne Roland. Sheller and Harsht she had said in her slurred speech. He had taken it for Sellert and Hart, not Heller and Hart.

Brandon's anger flared again and his body tensed. Elaine felt him go stiff and sensed what he was about to do. As Brandon's fist leaped upward, Elaine turned quickly, her hand catching it as she stared into his eyes. Then he relaxed and his fist dropped to his side.

Heller saw the movements and his derisive leer told them what he thought of Brandon and Elaine. "And I'd do it again," he said.

"Why, Jason?" she asked in a level tone.

"Because of who you are. Because you stole Tom's job."

"Sellert? What do you care about him?" she asked, shocked at his response.

"He's my stepbrother, and he's a damned fine producer!" Heller shouted as several police cars pulled up to the crowd, their lights flashing wildly, brought to the scene, Elaine supposed, by the FAA's radio monitoring, but that was the least of what was running through her mind.

Elaine kept staring at him, unable to believe that he could have acted so friendly to her while he was trying to destroy her. Then Brandon's arm settled around her shoulders. She turned to him and saw the love pouring from his eyes before she turned to face Heller again.

"I still can't believe you and Hart would try to kill someone just to get me off a picture," Elaine said quietly.

Heller glanced quickly at Hart but didn't say a word.

Brandon shook his head slowly at both men. "You're going to jail," he told them.

"No!" Hart cried. "We didn't sabotage the winch! That was an accident. Damn you!" he screamed at Heller. "You and Sellert said that no one would be hurt!"

Jason Heller's face turned pale as he looked around at the angry, pitying faces that stared at him. "No one was supposed to be hurt," Jason admitted in a whisper. "The copter was supposed to be damaged, that's all. The fuel line should have become clogged before the stuntman got onto the cable."

Then the police were there, and both Hart and Heller were being led away.

Brandon guided Elaine away from the crowd. Then, pulling her into his arms, he kissed her.

"Lanie, I think we can bring our relationship into the open now," he said with a smile, remembering the words she'd screamed to him when he was hanging in the air.

"Really?" she asked, matching his smile with her own. "Does that mean you're going to make an honest woman of me?" Elaine could have bitten her tongue the minute the words were out. "Brandon—"

"Hush," he said, cutting her protest short. "I will, but, as Chick said earlier, 'on one condition.'"

"Really? Is that a threat?"

"Lanie," he said in a low growl.

"What's the condition?"

"That you tell me how you knew it was Jason Heller. Dammit, I've spent every minute of my free time in the last few weeks trying to find out who was behind these incidents. I wouldn't have tried so hard if I'd known you'd already found out."

"But I hadn't," Elaine said as she raised her hand to stroke his face. "I only realized it after everyone had left."

Reaching into her pockets, Elaine drew out the spark plug that Chick had found. Speaking quickly, she explained what they had discovered, and how she'd realized what would happen to Brandon's helicopter.

"But how did you know it was Jason?" Brandon asked again.

"Jason was a hard worker, but he was also a typical producer type. He liked to give orders. He was efficient, and he was good, but he was never one to get his hands dirty. When I was speaking to him earlier, he waved good-bye to me. I saw several dark patches on his hand and fingers, but I didn't pay any attention to them. It was only when I looked at my own fingers after I touched the stain on the ground under the copter that I realized it had to have been him."

"Lanie, you're a hell of a detective," Brandon whispered.

"No, just a woman in love."

"Then I take it you'll let me make 'an honest woman' of you?"

"Only if you promise not to let any strange women pick you up on the Brooklyn Bridge," she whispered as his lips reached hers, and her heart began to pound in that wonderful way that could only be caused by Brandon.